CAST A BLUE SHADOW

Other Ohio Amish Mysteries by P. L. Gaus:

Blood of the Prodigal
Broken English
Clouds without Rain

CAST
A BLUE
SHADOW

AN OHIO AMISH MYSTERY

P. L. Gaus

Ohio University Press
Athens

Ohio University Press, Athens, Ohio 45701
© 2003 by P. L. Gaus

Printed in the United States of America
All rights reserved

Ohio University Press books are printed on acid-free paper ⊗ ™

15 14 12 11 10 09   5 4 3

Library of Congress Cataloging-in-Publication Data
Gaus, Paul L.
   Cast a blue shadow: an Ohio Amish mystery / P.L. Gaus.
     p. cm.
   ISBN 0-8214-1529-8 (cloth : alk. paper) — ISBN 0-8214-1530-1 (paper :
alk. paper)
      1. Amish Country (Ohio)—Fiction. 2. College teachers—Fiction.
3. Amish—Fiction. 4. Ohio—Fiction. I. Title.

   PS3557.A9517C37 2003
   813'.54—dc22

                                                     2003058094

For Laura and Amy, and dedicated to
my father, Robert L. Gaus, 1924–2002,
one of the quiet heroes of the twentieth
century.

Preface

ALL of the characters in this novel are purely fictional, and any apparent resemblance to people living or dead is entirely coincidental. The Holmes County setting for this story is authentic, but Millersburg College is fictional.

The sensational trial of an Amish midwife in Holmes County at time of press was not used as a model for anything in the present story, and no similarities with, or conclusions about, this trial or the people involved are intended.

The author wishes to thank his editors, David Sanders for insight, and Nancy Basmajian for vast expertise. Also, appreciation is due to the many fine professionals at Ohio University Press, an institution of great charm and grace, because of those who labor there. Thanks also to Pastor Dean Troyer, Heyl Road Church of Christ, Wooster, Ohio.

I Timothy 6:10

For the love of money is a root of all kinds of evil.
Some people, eager for money, have wandered from
the faith and pierced their hearts with many griefs.

I am always humbled by the infinite ingenuity of the
Lord, who can make a red barn cast a blue shadow.

—E. B. White

CAST A BLUE SHADOW

1

Saturday, November 2
Dawn, Holmes County, Ohio

CURLED up in her black down parka, Martha Lehman lay on her side, back pressed firmly against the polished wood door, knees drawn tightly to her chest. The white block lettering on the door read Dr. Evelyn White Carson, Psychiatrist. Martha was aware only of the rough, cold carpet pressing into her cheek and of long, ragged breaths that repeatedly dragged her out of a trance. Thus, for an hour, before sunrise bled pink hues through the window at the end of the second-floor hall, she lay in a stupor, hounded again by a dreadful loneliness.

In wakeful moments, with a fervor born of an all-too-familiar pain, she renewed a childhood vow. Silence, she thought, had never betrayed her, and it was Silence she'd cling to now. Silence had brought her to Dr. Carson as a child, and Silence she would trust again. Then, it had been Carson who had understood the wordlessness. The sorrow and isolation of a mute child. It will be Carson, now, she prayed, who will remember.

Thoughts formed only intermittently, in a cold, tortured nightmare of helplessness.

Silence again, she vowed—now, more than ever before. The snap and pop of blue cotton shirts and black denim vests in a stiff winter breeze, clutching at her from a clothesline.

Alone again, and safe that way. Menacing, cracked lips that sternly mouthed, "Save your little sisters." A childhood nightmare, empowered, somehow, to hurt her again.

How had She known? A man's blue shirt tore loose from the clothesline, enveloped her face, and smothered her, its weight unbearable, its odor a familiar horror. On weak child's legs, she struggled to carry the burden of an adult, and managed to breathe only in gasps.

Too soon for Her to have known it. And yet She had. The wind began to whisper judgment from the clothesline. Shirt sleeves snapping near her eyes. Wagging fingers, all of them.

Fallen like Babylon, Martha Lehman. "So, choose, young Martha," an urgent voice pleaded. "Choose the better way."

Sonny, what have you done? The frowning congregation walked out of the barn, all their faces down, all their backs turned. No one dared to believe it possible. To accept the hell it signified.

What plans now? He's lost to you. No place for plain girls in his murderous world. Nor any place in the old. No haven for outcast girls.

The cold tracks of tears on her cheeks slowly awakened her. She unclasped her knees and felt a binding stickiness between her fingers. Unzipping her parka, she instinctively pressed her palms to her belly and felt the stickiness there, too. Sitting up, she brushed hair from her eyes, smearing her forehead. She looked down in confusion and saw her white lace apron stained dark red. Gasping, she fell back on her side, knotting her fingers into the bloody fabric.

Vaguely, now, she recalled brief snatches of last night's disastrous conversation with Sonny's mother. She dimly remembered driving away in the snow. A sleepless night of confusion and frustration. Her decision to go back. The blood. Running. Fleeing in the storm.

But these were indistinct memories. Perhaps more dreams, she thought, as she lay motionless. Mere impressions. As if her mind had conjured events that her heart could not allow.

2

Friday, November 1
6:00 P.M.

THE ALBERTA clipper cut into Holmes County right when the weather crew on FOX 8 News in Cleveland had predicted it would. A hint of morning sun had earlier given way to gray skies, and the temperature had dropped twenty degrees by 9:00 A.M. By noon, most of the Amish settlements had six to eight inches of new snow on the ground, and buggies were traded for sleighs throughout the region. By evening, the clipper had pushed east, and moist air from the south blended sleet with the blowing snow, adding another four inches or so to the mix. Snowplows, active all day, still had not cleared the secondary roads by dusk, and the sheriff's office issued a travel advisory. As night fell, Amish farmers bedded down livestock, latched barns tight, stoked fires in wood stoves, and gathered their families inside.

Sheltered from the storm, Juliet Favor pushed open the lid of her tanning bed, swung her slender legs out to the floor, and stood up on the heated redwood planks of her third-floor gym-sauna. She took a royal blue towel from a gold hook on the wall and crossed to the mirrors on the other side of the warm attic room. Nude, as she dried her arms and breasts, she studied her tan in the floor-to-ceiling glass. She had every right to be pleased with what she saw, but a too critical eye for matters physical failed to recognize the true beauty in her form. For Juliet Favor, the tan had only momentarily been adequate.

July and August in the Mediterranean had laid down a deep copper hue. In the salons of Paris, between this year's strategic nips and tucks, she had managed to hold most of her color. October in Rio had deepened her copper to a bronze that she had thought would last for months.

But tonight, assessing her reflection, she shook her head and muttered a curse. Stay in the States for another two weeks, she thought, and you'll have no color left for Jamaica.

So, be done with Ohio. Wrap it all up. Tomorrow, if possible. Let them squirm, the whole lot of them. Dominate as Harry always had. They hadn't deserved Favor money for years.

Closer to the mirrors, Juliet lifted artfully colored blond hair behind her left ear and ran a finger lightly along the skin where an incision had been made. She felt nothing unusual, and smiled. She pulled the other ear forward and peered sideways into the mirror. Nothing there either, she saw with approval. Dr. Verheit of Paris—you do such nice work. On this point, she could afford to be congratulatory. Where else but Paris for those little fixes that kept a woman of fifty-three looking not a day over forty?

She was diminutive and proportioned well. Her narrow face was pleasant enough when a rare smile found a home there. To new acquaintances, aging seemed to have ignored Juliet Favor. The truth, as old friends knew, was that she had anticipated its advances skillfully.

She turned left and right in front of the mirrors and smiled briefly. Then she stepped into the recessed space where one of six large dormer windows faced west.

The season's first bitter storm blew snow and sleet against the glass, and the roofline carried a mournful tune as the wind played its music on the gutters outside. Winter air penetrated the seams of the window, and she felt the blizzard's chill near the floor, on the tops of her bare feet. Eyes closed, she dropped the towel over her toes and stiffened, pulling pins from her hair to let it down over her shoulders. She fluffed her hair with thin fingers and shook it out fuller. Eyes open, she shuffled closer to the windowpane, stood on tiptoes, and looked out warily at the storm. With her forehead pressed against the cold glass, she studied the service drive far below. White flurries danced brightly in the floodlights, and she saw snow drifting in high mounds along a line of bushes on the west side of the mansion. After a quick assessment, she retreated from the window and wrapped the towel tightly around her chest.

From a stainless steel rack in the center of the large exercise room, Favor selected two five-pound free weights. On the other side of the room, near the stairs that led down to her second-floor master bath, she leaned a shoulder against an intercom button as she flexed one arm and then the other, waiting for her butler's reply. In short order, "Yes, Ms. Favor" came from a deep, calm voice through the speaker on the wall.

"Daniel," she scolded, "you know I hate snow. Turn off the floodlights."

"Right away, Ms. Favor."

"Damn it, Daniel, were you trying to annoy me?"

"No, ma'am."

"Then turn out those lights!"

"At once."

"Wait. What have you laid out for me?"

"Oh, just a few frumpy old things, ma'am."

"Knock it off, Daniel," she said, pumping her arms faster now, and smiling.

"A gray pants suit with a red carnation, and a peach and rose chiffon evening gown with a low neckline."

"Perfect, Daniel. We start at 8:00. Right?"

"7:30, Ms. Favor. Sonny called for an appointment."

"What's he want? He knows I'll see him in New York."

"As he explained it to me, ma'am, he'll be introducing a young lady from the college."

"Sonny's got a girl?"

"Apparently so."

"Humph. If you say so," Favor said, pumping the weights very slowly now. "Then switch to a blue business suit with a short skirt, Daniel."

"Will you require assistance dressing tonight, Ms. Favor?"

"Of course, Daniel. Please draw my bath. I'll be down in fifteen minutes."

Favor switched off the intercom, dropped her blue towel, and padded across the soft redwood flooring to an antique cherry vanity beside a treadmill. From the top drawer she took out one of a dozen pairs of her late husband's boxer shorts and stepped into them, snapping the elastic at her waist. From the second drawer, she chose a white sports bra. She slipped into it, and bent over at the waist to adjust herself in front.

The floodlights outside switched off, and the windows went dark. She thumbed down a light switch on the wall beside her, and the room darkened, too. Stepping onto the treadmill, she stared at the glass in a south-facing window. Now the only light in the room came from the red and green display on the panel in front of her, reflected in the windowpane. She paced vigorously on the machine, her eyes registering only vague patches of color as she thought in the dark about the people the evening would bring. First, a college president, so exasperatingly pliable. What had she ever seen in him? Professors—so completely absorbed in their academic lives. So dull and myopic, as Harry had always said. But there were the better ones. Passionate, resourceful, and principled. Deans and chairpersons, too. Some keepers there, to be sure. And if some served as play toys over the years—who cared?

But Sonny—what a disappointment. He'd never be the equal of his father. So, face up to that now, she mused despondently.

And Harry. God, what a man he had been! It had been six years, now. Six years and seven months, or something near that, anyway. There had been so much left to do.

But never mind. He had given her his legacy in time to make

a difference. To dominate. To manage a fortune. She had always thought that her marriage to Harry Newton Favor would be the only thing that could ever matter to her. But, oh, how wrong!

She was running now, sweating lightly and smiling. Through superb conditioning, she had passed rapidly into her runner's endorphin zone, where, for her, there was always a clear and sustaining vision of purpose.

Fortune.

Wealth.

Money—the only reliable commodity.

A vehicle for power, to be sure, but also a surpassing comfort just to have it. To grow it. Money enabled everything in her life. It was a means, a resource, a currency. And used properly, it could be transformed into anything. Possessions. Health and vitality. Power. Travel. Even time. Money bought time for everything.

But using it was only scant half to its greater challenge—keeping it. The simple possession of wealth, Juliet Favor figured, was key to this world and all it held. She had learned this hard lesson as a poor girl. True, it could buy anything, take her anywhere, set her free with all the time she needed. It garnered influence and power. That we'll see tonight, she thought. But having and holding wealth gave the truest joys. To use it, yes, obviously. But to have it, to keep it—that transcends it all. Most people never understood that. Wealth had long ago become both the foundation and the stronghold of her soul. And this was the legacy she intended to leave her children. Well, at least her son. If he proved equal to the task.

AT AN oval dressing mirror, Juliet Favor watched as Daniel Bliss pinned the red carnation to the lapel of her blazer. He was a tall, thin, elderly gentleman dressed in a tuxedo. His white hair was brushed back and lay close to his scalp. His angular face was accented by high cheekbones and thin lips. Gray eyes watched Juliet attentively, but with a practiced, reserved disinterest.

"Have you prepared both pitchers of drinks?" she asked.

"Yes," Daniel replied. "Yours is the green Tiffany. The Waterford is for everyone else."

"Sonny is here?"

"In the parlor, ma'am."

"Set up in the bar, Daniel, and take them in there. I'll be down shortly."

"We're on the clock, ma'am," Daniel remarked.

"I know that well enough," Favor replied, reaching up to pat the butler's cheek playfully. "I want her to cool her heels a bit. Fix them both up with drinks, Daniel. We don't want to be inhospitable."

"Very well, ma'am, but I doubt she'll have one," Daniel said.

"What's that supposed to mean?"

"You'll see," Daniel replied and walked out into the hallway to take the grand staircase to the first floor.

Favor watched the time carefully and descended at 7:38 P.M. In the bar, she found her son in blue jeans and a green-and-white Millersburg College sweatshirt. He crossed the room to his mother and attempted to embrace her, but she held him stiffly by the shoulders and permitted only a brief, formal kiss on her cheek.

"You disappoint me, Sonny. Surely you can dress better than this for such an occasion."

Sonny Favor blushed. His gaze fell to the floor, and, glancing anxiously at a young girl in plain dress, he knew she had seen his shame. "Mom, I'd like you to meet Martha Lehman," he managed to say.

At the teak and walnut bar, Juliet Favor poured a drink and remarked, "Now there is a girl who can dress for an occasion."

Martha Lehman stood with good posture and a hopeful smile at the other end of the ornate bar. On her head was a white lace prayer cap. Her brown hair was up in a Mennonite bun. Her cotton blouse was light pink with white buttons, and her long skirt was forest green. Over those, she wore a white apron, tied behind her neck and waist. She had on black hose and black string-tie shoes. A small pair of wire-rimmed glasses accented her eyes, which were blue. Her cheeks flushed rose as Favor turned to appraise her from head to toe.

"Miss Lerman," Favor said and came along the bar holding out her hand.

"It's Lehman," Martha said. "Martha. And how do you do, Mrs. Favor?"

"Ms. Favor," Juliet said with a smile.

"Ms. Favor, then," Martha greeted again and turned her eyes nervously to Sonny. "How do you do."

"That remains to be seen," Favor said and asked, "You're not having anything to drink, Martha?"

Sonny and Martha stepped away from the bar and held hands. Favor turned her back to them, drained her glass, and poured another drink from the green Tiffany pitcher. Still with her back turned, she watched them in the mirror behind the bar and said, "I presume you've found time for your studies, Sonny. Has he, Martha?" She turned slowly to them and added, "You have been letting Sonny study some, now, haven't you, young Martha Lehman?"

Martha blushed and started to say something. Sonny spoke up. "I've been studying plenty, Mother. Got at least a B in 'most everything."

"'Most everything'! Sonny, where in the world did you learn to talk? Favors are raised to do better."

"Almost everything," Sonny corrected.

"And some C's, no doubt."

"I'm doin' fine," Sonny said weakly.

"Sonny, Sonny," Favor said disapprovingly and sipped at her drink.

Sonny was a large, plump boy with black hair and rosy cheeks. He held himself erect for the most part, the result of long years of training in private schools. Now, though, his shoulders had rounded and slumped. He nervously shifted his weight and let go of Martha's hand, as if he had forgotten she was there.

Favor came forward slowly, reached up to rest a gentle hand on Sonny's shoulder, watched his downcast eyes for a moment, and said, "We Favors look for A's. What would Daddy think?"

Sonny shrugged and tried to hide his embarrassment by avoiding the eyes of both women. His shoulders seemed to carry a heavy yet familiar burden.

"Now, Sonny," Favor said. "Step into the parlor so Martha and I can talk. I'll bring her out to you."

AFTER a long, appraising silence, Juliet Favor said to Martha Lehman, "I presume, Martha, that your costume signifies some religious sect."

"It's Mennonite, ma'am," Martha replied.

"Not Amish? I hope you're not one of those backward country girls. Sonny's future can harbor none of that."

Taken aback, Martha managed only, "Ma'am?"

"I have plans for Sonny, Martha. You can appreciate that, I'm sure. I've known plenty of trashy country girls who figured on breeding their way into wealth."

Martha took a step forward and defended herself. "My family is conservative Mennonite. I see no reason to apologize for that. It's a sect derived from the old Black Bumper Amish."

"Black Bumper Amish?" Juliet repeated, intrigued despite herself.

"Yes. They drove cars, but painted the bumpers and shiny metal parts flat black. But, even if I were Amish, you have no reason to fear my relationship with Sonny."

"Fear? My dear girl, I assure you I do not fear anything about you. You may be in college, but you're still just a plain country girl with designs on my boy. You know our family has money."

Martha, unsettled, made no reply.

Juliet Favor stepped up to Martha, a scant five inches from her face, and continued talking softly, taking satisfaction that Martha's eyes sought the carpet at her feet, and that her cheeks and ears flamed red.

IT TOOK no more than six minutes. Martha came alone to Sonny in the parlor with pools in her eyes. She looked at him with a lost expression, and the tears spilled out onto her cheeks. He embraced her, feeling more confused than sorry.

"Mom's not so bad once you get to know her," he said awkwardly. "She thinks of family, first. Duty, obligations, her 'legacy.' Give her a chance, Martha. She's had it rough since Dad died, and I think she overcompensates."

SONNY left Martha in the parlor and came back nervously through the main foyer, where a grand staircase led to the second-floor hallway with the master bath and bedroom. This was the front staircase. A rear one led from the kitchen at the back of the house to a second-floor vestibule with two bedrooms, each with an attached bath.

Sonny crossed in front of the main stairs and marched across the marble floor, into the bar. Passing through, he entered a library and turned left to take a door to Daniel's office and prep room adjoining the formal dining room on the other side. He found his mother there with the butler, in a long, narrow room, which Daniel had fitted with a small desk and a laptop, china and crystal cabinets, and a chest for silver service. There were also prep tables for dinners, and a tall refrigerator with glass doors, holding beverages of all descriptions. A wet bar stood against the wall beside the refrigerator. The narrow aisle down the middle of the room was wide enough for only two people to pass comfortably.

Favor poured herself another drink as Sonny squeezed past her and took a 7 UP from the refrigerator. Juliet sipped her drink slowly and appraised her son carefully. Daniel stood silently at the far end of the narrow room, by the swinging doors to the kitchen and pantries beyond.

Eventually, Sonny managed to ask, "What did you say to her, Mom?"

"Why, nothing at all, really, Sonny. Of course I wanted her to know how important your studies are to us. You'd agree to that, wouldn't you?"

"I guess so, if that was all."

"Of course. Now, what's the problem?"

"She's crying."

"She's the emotional type, Sonny. I saw that right away. She'll be fine."

"I've never seen her so upset," Sonny said, confused by his emotions. He felt guilty again, but did not understand why. It seemed to him that he had often felt this way, even as a child, and that he had, in some unnatural way, grown accustomed to it. "I want you to like her, Mom."

"I'm sure I will, Sonny. Now don't leave the poor thing alone too long."

Sonny looked to Daniel for reassurance, but Daniel avoided his gaze.

Favor let a moment pass as she sipped her drink, and then she took her son by the arm, escorted him back into the library, and headed him toward the front parlor. Back in Daniel's room, she said, "That kid's going to need nursemaiding all his life."

"He's still young, Ms. Favor," Daniel said.

"He's a spineless dope. Not recognizable as Harry's son," she muttered, squeezing her temples between thumb and forefinger. She rubbed at the back of her neck, eyes shut tight. "You call Dick Pomeroy?" she asked, weakly. "I'm out of medicine."

"Professor Pomeroy will arrive ahead of the others."

"Good," Favor said, with her eyes still closed. "DiSalvo is next, right?"

"He's due any minute."

"Show him into the parlor."

"Sonny and his young lady are probably still there."

"I know that!" Favor snapped. "I want Sonny to hear that I'm changing my will. Want to see if that will snap him around."

"You've got DiSalvo until 8:20, and then it's President Laughton."

"Him you can leave in the foyer," Favor schemed. "It'll serve him right for opposing me on the board. Let him hold his hat for a good ten minutes in the front foyer. I want you to leave the doors to the parlor open so he can see me working with DiSalvo. I'll take Laughton into the bar, then, when I think he's heard enough. You be sure Sonny gets there too, if I don't have him with me then. And please see to DiSalvo while I'm talking to Laughton. He gets hungry, so please bring him something."

"I do recall, ma'am. I'll see that he's taken care of."

HENRY DiSalvo pushed his boots through the white drifts on the steps to the wraparound front porch. The porch was lighted brightly by several hanging fixtures, but he had walked the last fifty yards up the drive in the dark. His face and glasses had been pelted with snow and sleet, and his long black coat was plastered white in front. He rang the door chimes, and Daniel, waiting for him inside, opened the doors immediately. DiSalvo brushed off his overcoat before entering, and, once he was inside with the doors closed, Daniel took his coat, gloves, and hat.

From a briefcase, DiSalvo took out a pair of brown penny loafers and stood, first on one foot and then on the other, to pull off hiking boots and put on the loafers. Daniel steadied the elderly gentleman by holding his arm.

"We are serving martinis and hors d'oeuvres now," Daniel said, "and Madam hopes you'll stay for dinner later this evening."

"I could use a drink," DiSalvo replied. "And Daniel, I had to leave my car about halfway down the drive. Stuck in the snow, I'm afraid."

"I'll see to it," Daniel said. "Ms. Favor will join you in the parlor, Mr. DiSalvo."

DiSalvo handed Daniel the keys to his car, and, knowing the house well, took the doors to his left, went into the spacious parlor, and walked to the far wall, by the fireplace. As he warmed himself at the wood fire, his eyes wandered along the mantel where several tall baseball trophies flanked a squat brass trophy depicting the low scrummage of a rugby team. He tilted the trophy back, bent his head low, and read the inscription on the bottom:

> *Ohio Athletic Conference*
> *1970 Champions*
> *Millersburg College*
> *Henry Luke DiSalvo, Coach*
> *Harry Newton Favor, Captain*

He eased the trophy into place, turned his back to the fire, and reacquainted himself with the Favor parlor. The decor was French Provincial, and DiSalvo knew some of the smaller armchairs to be authentic Louis XIV. The long drapes on the front window had been chosen by his wife in France, twenty years ago, when the DiSalvos had vacationed with the Favors on the Continent. His Elaine was gone now, and so was Harry Favor. Feeling melancholy, he took a seat in front of the windows, on a divan covered in yellow flowered fabric. He opened his briefcase, set a black Thinkpad across his knees, and punched up the documents in the Juliet Favor account. From the file menu, he chose the second document on the list, Last Will and Testament. He began proofreading out of habit.

Soon Daniel reappeared with a silver tray of martinis and canapés and announced Favor and her son. Favor entered the room with an expansive sweep of her arms and said, "Tonight, Henry! All the details ready?"

"Right here," DiSalvo replied and tapped the screen on his laptop. Awkwardly, he tried to rise to his feet holding the laptop open, and Favor said, "For God's sake, Henry, sit down."

DiSalvo dropped back onto the divan and said, "Tonight we'll finalize, and by tomorrow I'll have all the documents prepared for your signature. My calendar is yours for the entire day."

"We should be done by 4:00," Favor said. "They're all going to try to see me early, I'm sure, but Daniel knows the appointment schedule. You've got Sunday scheduled for the second group, too?"

"Yes. The other academic departments," DiSalvo said. "Those from Saturday's banquet."

Daniel crossed the room to DiSalvo and bent deferentially to offer the tray to the lawyer. DiSalvo selected a plate of crackers and pâté, which he set on an antique table beside the divan. He also took a martini and sipped lightly before setting the glass on a silver coaster next to the plate.

"Take a seat next to Mr. DiSalvo there, Sonny," Favor instructed. "We've matters to discuss."

"I want to call to see if Martha got home all right," Sonny answered and turned to the door.

"Nonsense!" Favor barked. "Sit down and sit down now, Sonny." Her eyes narrowed fiercely, and to cover her irritation, she stepped to the windows to make a show of adjusting the curtains. There she glanced out briefly at sleet raking the front porch, and sighed heavily.

"Where's your Lexus, Sonny?" Favor demanded and turned to see her son taking a seat on a delicate antique chair. "Not the Louis XIV, Sonny! Show some common sense, will you. I swear, Daniel, show Junior where to sit."

She turned back to look out the front parlor windows, and Sonny caught a reflection of her expression in the window glass. His eyes tipped to the carpet. "Martha took the car," he muttered.

Spinning around, Juliet said, "You're going to have to plow, Daniel. Too many people tonight not to plow it out at least once."

"Right away, Ms. Favor," Daniel answered. He set the martini tray on a round table with maple inlays near the fireplace and left through an ornate door to the large dining room.

"Sonny, I expected better from you, bringing a Plain Jane like that to see me. And to let her drive your Lexus! What's wrong with your head?"

"She wanted to go back to town in the worst way, Mom. What did you say to her?" Sonny asked, taking a seat next to DiSalvo.

"She could have gotten a ride back with any of a dozen people tonight."

"I didn't know that, Mom."

"You didn't ask."

"I hope you didn't hurt her feelings."

"I've got plans for you, Sonny. Don't make me think that you're not ready."

Confused by his emotions, Sonny glanced nervously at DiSalvo.

His mother said, "You are supposed to move into the business, Sonny. Now I'm not sure you'll measure up." She drained her martini glass and crossed the room to pour another drink from her green pitcher.

"What are you talking about?" Sonny asked.

"I'm reorganizing the whole estate," she replied. "Why do you think Mr. DiSalvo is here?"

Instinctively, Sonny reached for an anchor. "I've got a trust fund. I'll have that in three years, and you can't touch it."

"True, Sonny. The trust is yours. Your sister's is the same, but it was supposed to go to her next month."

Sonny stood up and paced in front of the divan.

With slow, deliberate words, Juliet said, "I still have the authority to delay both your trusts until you're thirty, if I don't like the progress you've made."

"You wouldn't," Sonny said and stopped pacing to face his mother at the fireplace.

Juliet Favor sipped her drink, looked at her son over the top of her glass, and said, "Henry."

DiSalvo pulled up another document on his screen and read, "I, Juliet Favor, deem that Sally Newton Favor is not presently competent to take responsibility for the trust left her by my late husband, Harry Newton Favor, and I do hereby suspend implementation of said Trust until her thirtieth birthday."

"That means, Sonny," Juliet explained, "that Sally is going to have to get by on an allowance of $4,000 a month until she is thirty."

"You wouldn't," Sonny repeated, less confidently.

"Who's her current lover?" Favor asked.

"You know, Mom."

"Exactly. We're not going to have that sort of thing among the Favors."

"You've got no right to control her life like that, Mom."

"I am simply delaying the onset of her trust. Perhaps she'll change her mind."

"What about Martha?"

"Don't be silly. I won't hear you talk this way."

"What are you gonna do, Mom? Take away my trust too?"

Favor pointed a finger at the laptop.

DiSalvo chose another document and began to read. "I, Juliet Favor, deem that Samuel 'Sonny' Newton Favor is not competent . . ."

"Stop it!" Sonny shouted, arms stiff at his sides and eyes watering.

Pointing at DiSalvo's laptop, Favor hissed, "Dump that Mennonite loser, or I'll sign it. I swear I will, Sonny."

Sonny froze in the center of the parlor, back straight, arms to his sides, making impotent fists. DiSalvo blushed for the boy and closed the laptop slowly. Juliet walked to Sonny and lightly embraced him. He stiffened. She took a step back, rested her left hand gently on his shoulder, and lifted his chin with the slender, tanned fingers of her right hand.

"Listen to me, Sonny. You've no idea how vast your father's fortune really is. How vast mine is. And yours, if you measure up. Daddy always meant to bring you along himself, but he didn't live that long, did he? Instead, when he knew he was ill, when you were eight, he began training me. So that I could be there when you came of age. Now you're already a freshman. That gives us only

three years. You're going to have to excel at your studies. I'll demand an MBA after college. I have Harvard in mind, and I've already started working on that. Your grades aren't going to be that
good if high school is any indication, so you'll need my help then,
as usual, and it's time I laid the groundwork for that. No matter,
it's already in the works. But you'll have to spend summers with
me, learning how to manage the wealth. It's not just money, Sonny.
It's holdings, directorships, chairmanships—a conglomerate you'll
never understand unless we start now."

"What about what *I* want?" Sonny asked weakly.

"What *you* want? I'm *talking* about you, Sonny!" Favor shouted
and shook his shoulders. "Henry, put it all on your screen there."

DiSalvo stroked the keys of his laptop, and Juliet led her son to
a seat beside the lawyer. On the screen, Sonny read an outline of his
future. Board memberships in three companies upon graduation.
Directorships after an MBA. CEO of one company at twenty-eight.
More positions and responsibilities with each coming year. And
last, when his mother was gone, complete control of the Favor fortune. The enormity of the plan staggered him, and he could not
think clearly. His mind struggled with the notion that so much had
been planned for him, and he felt caged. He wondered, briefly, how
Martha Lehman would fit into such a life.

"Sonny," Juliet said and sat down beside him. "Sonny, listen.

"You've been sheltered, Sonny. Now it's time you faced the des-
tiny your father and I have laid out for you. Wealth is more than
money. It's the one asset that rises above all others. It's the only reliable commodity this world has to offer. It is the supreme commodity, Sonny, and you've got to learn to handle it. Oh, it takes
many forms, and you'll have to start learning about that. But Sonny,
everything you'll want in life derives from wealth. Your estate. Free-
dom. Power and choice. These all lie subordinate to the one thing
that drives them all—raw, fabulous wealth."

Sonny sat for a long moment as if hypnotized. He eventually
stirred, and Juliet drew him to his feet.

"Now, Sonny," she said. "Many people will come and go tonight. I want you to stay close beside me. Follow me. Listen. Learn tonight, Sonny. I do it all for you. Life's a dance. It can be orchestrated. Watch me lead the first dance of wealth, Sonny—the Puppeteer's Waltz. You've got to learn to be a puppeteer if you're ever going to handle wealth properly."

3

Friday, November 1
8:30 P.M.

IN MILLERSBURG, Martha Lehman parked Sonny Favor's silver Lexus in the deep snow on the parking lot of Cal Troyer's little white church house. A ground light shined through the falling snow to illuminate the church sign: Church of Christ, Christian. Caleb Troyer, Pastor.

Martha dried her eyes and pushed the car door open, scraping the drifts aside with the bottom edge of the door. She stepped out and sank into the snow, soaking her hose and shoes. She folded her black parka closed in front by wrapping her arms across her chest and trudged, head down against the blowing snow, to the side door of the church building, which she found unlocked. Inside, she slipped out of her parka, took off her wet shoes, and sat in the dark sanctuary's first pew. She stared at the gold cross on the plain oak altar and tried to think. To formulate a plan.

Clearly her first meeting with Sonny's mother had been a disaster. What right did she have to talk that way? There seemed little point in going back. But even more troubling was Sonny's reaction. Or rather his lack of one. Send her away with his car? What had that been about? And not to have come with her?

Hurt as much as angry, Martha got up from the pew and paced in front of the altar. Frustrated, she stopped, looked at the cross, lifted her eyes to the ceiling, and shouted, "Why can't you let me be happy? I deserve to be happy!"

From the back of the sanctuary, Cal Troyer answered, "Looks like you've come to the right place, Martha."

Martha spun around and saw the short pastor coming slowly down the center aisle. "How long have you been there, Cal?" Martha asked.

"Just got here now," Cal said, removing his coat and stomping snow off his boots onto the carpet. "I saw a car in the parking lot."

His long white hair was tied in a ponytail. Calm eyes anchored his round face, and he smiled at her as he approached.

Martha, unnerved as usual by his peacefulness and grace, sat down and said, "Everything's falling apart, Cal. My boyfriend's mother hates me, and I can't sleep through the night. My professors aren't happy with my work anymore, and my parents think I'm a tramp. I just want to be happy, Cal. What's wrong with that?"

"Nothing at all," Cal said. He sat beside her and took her hands in his. "Maybe you and I need to pray about this."

"A lot of good that'll do," Martha said bitterly.

"I can't believe you mean that."

"Maybe I'm not the girl you think I am, Cal."

"You know you can talk to me," Cal said. "Any time, and about anything."

"I've lost my way."

"Is it really that bad?" Cal asked.

"Nothing's right anymore, Cal," Martha said. Tears formed in her eyes. "There's something wrong with me. Something really big. Something's broken, and I've known I wasn't normal for a long time. It's horrible. You wouldn't believe my nightmares. I can't get a minute's peace. I don't know. Everything goes rotten on me. School, friends. Boyfriend. Why does God hate me?"

"He doesn't," Cal said softly.

"Why can't I remember my childhood?"

Cal waited a beat, then said, "What do you mean?"

"My psychiatrist knows more about my childhood than I do."

"You weren't much of a talker, Martha."

"Yeah, but why? Something must have happened. From five or six to about nine, I can't remember a thing. After that, I did bad things, Cal. Still do."

"What does Dr. Carson say?"

"That I have issues. Something I haven't been able to face. She says when I'm ready to face it, I'll remember."

"Tell me about your nightmares."

"You'll think I'm nuts."

"I don't think so."

"It's always a blue shirt. An Amish shirt. Flies off a clothesline and wraps over my face so I can't breathe."

"That's it?"

"It's heavy, Cal. The shirt is heavy on me. It gets on top of me, and I can't breathe. Then all the other laundry on the line starts whispering. It's Amish laundry. Amish whispering. It all piles up on me. It's supposed to be light as a breeze, but I can't move. Can't get up. I'm gasping for air."

"Have you told anyone?"

"Just you."

"Dr. Carson could help."

"I don't want doctors anymore. Don't want to be sick anymore," Martha said, crying again. "Why can't I be normal?"

"We need to pray about this," Cal said.

"God doesn't answer my prayers."

"Have you tried?"

"Not lately."

"You ought to."

"God doesn't care about me. I've known that since I was a kid," Martha said and rose. There was a wild anger in her eyes.

She grabbed her parka off the pew, and then sat back down to put on her shoes. Getting up again, she said, "I'm in trouble, again, Cal. So you tell me. How has God ever cared even two cents for me?"

4

Friday, November 1
8:10 P.M.

JULIET Favor came back into the foyer squeezing her temples, and slowly climbed the grand staircase to the second floor. In the bathroom, she found a little glass bottle with a ground-glass stopper and carried it into the master bedroom, inverting the bottle to moisten the stopper. When she switched on the light, she found Sally Favor sprawled on the bed with her girlfriend in her arms. They both held champagne glasses, and they smiled at Favor and kissed.

Although her ears flushed crimson, Juliet Favor showed no other immediate reaction. She tilted her head back to let her hair fall away from her face and dabbed the wet glass stopper at each temple.

"That's just great, Sally," Favor said bitterly. "Rub my face in it."

"You remember Juliet, don't you, Jenny?" Sally taunted. "She's that trust-busting homophobe we call Mom."

"Bitch!" Favor hissed.

"Takes one to know one, Mommy Dearest," Sally Favor replied spitefully, her speech slurred. She drained her champagne and threw the empty glass onto the carpet, where the stem broke with a muted "tink."

Juliet Favor dabbed at her temples again and rubbed the clear liquid in with her thumbs. "Your trust is suspended, Sally. But I guess you already know that."

"I can hire a lawyer, too," Sally said. She took the second glass from Jenny, drank it down defiantly, and tossed it onto the carpet beside the first one. Then she pulled Jenny off the bed to stand face to face with her mother. "Why don't you just go ahead and castrate him, Mother? I'm sure you know you're raising a eunuch as it is."

Favor pushed her daughter away and headed for the staircase.

Drunk, Sally listed like a ship whose cargo had broken loose in the hold. She steadied herself against a dresser, recovered, and led her lover by the hand down the staircase too rapidly, following her mother carelessly. They stumbled on the steps and grabbed for the banister near the bottom of the staircase. Once down in the foyer, Sally inquired mockingly, "Do we have another headache, Mommy? Professor Pomeroy's little miracle bottle almost empty?"

Favor retreated into the bar and then the library, and leaned over with both palms flat on a large reading table, eyes closed, feeling pressure and pain rise in the back of her neck.

Sally entered the paneled library with her arm around Jenny, spun around with her, and ushered her into the adjoining butler's room, where they poured the two last drinks from a champagne bottle before clanging the empty into a wastebasket beside Daniel's desk.

Favor charged after them and said, "Since you two must have been eavesdropping, you'll know I explained to Sonny that I can do whatever I want with your trusts."

Sally made a show of kissing Jenny hard on the lips, lifted her glass high, and shouted, "There's more to life than money, Mother!"

"Get out!" Favor screamed.

"Screw you, Mom."

"You're a disgrace!"

"Like I care what you think."

"I'm calling the police."

"Don't bother," Sally said and pushed with Jenny through the swinging doors into the kitchen.

Favor snatched a cordless phone from Daniel's desk and followed. She found the two women struggling into winter coats, and, with a forced show of calm, went back slowly through the swinging doors.

JULIET found her little bottle of medicine in the bedroom and dabbed anxiously at her temples. Frustrated, she eyed the bottle, saw that it was empty, and threw it into a corner of the room. At the wall-mounted intercom, she rang impatiently for Daniel several times. No answer. She rubbed the back of her neck and moved slowly to a front window to peer out. Normally, that window gave a view of a long, curving, blacktop driveway that led down to the north side of Route 39, seven miles west of Millersburg. Tonight, she saw only a blinding blizzard of white. It unnerved her, and, feeling trapped, she retrieved the medicine bottle from the corner of the room. Suffering, with the bottle inverted close to her eyes, she tried to wet the stopper with a film of the thick liquid, but the bottle was truly empty.

In the master bathroom, Favor pulled medicines and perfumes from the medicine cabinet and cast them angrily to the floor. Pawing now, in the back of the cabinet she found an old bottle that still held some of the clear and colorless liquid. She rubbed the stopper against her temples and leaned over at the sink to calm herself. After a moment, with her balance restored, she tried the wall intercom again, with no result. She heard a faint growl outside and went back to the bedroom window to see Daniel below, on a small tractor in driving snow, plowing the blacktop circle in front of the house. Resigned for the moment, Favor got the last bit of medicine out and then composed herself to descend the staircase.

In the parlor with her lawyer DiSalvo, she busied herself for the next several minutes with the various documents they were to finalize. When she heard Daniel at the back door, she excused herself, left through the door to the dining room, and found her butler in the pantry at the back of the house.

"I'm out of medicine," she said directly, pulling the butler aside, out of earshot of the cooks.

"Already?" Daniel asked and hung a long black dress coat on a peg beside the back door. He watched her close her eyes and rub her neck and said, "Pomeroy didn't give you his new bottle?"

"No," Favor replied in exasperation.

"I sent him up."

"Never saw him."

"He just went up. I'm surprised you didn't see him."

"I came through the dining room."

"Wait right here, if you please," Daniel said and went quickly up the back staircase to the second floor. Shortly, he returned, carrying a fresh stoppered bottle. "He put it on your dresser, ma'am."

Grateful, Favor took the little bottle in both hands and closed her eyes as if meditating. She dabbed more of the liquid on her temples, and after composing herself, said, "OK, then. Please put this back in the bedroom. I'm afraid I left quite a mess in the bathroom."

"I will attend to it, ma'am," Daniel replied.

She handed over the bottle as if it were of immense value and said, "I'll be with DiSalvo when Laughton arrives. But I'm not going to change first. We'll have to do that later, Daniel."

5

Friday, November 1
8:45 P.M.

MARTHA swiped her plastic night pass through the magnetic reader at her dorm's front entrance, pulled the heavy oak door open, and climbed the stairs to her third-floor suite. She pushed through the door, switched on the lights, and startled her roommate, who was tangled in the arms of her boyfriend on the couch, finishing a joint. Her roommate, only mildly embarrassed, grumbled, "Turn out the lights, would you."

Martha switched off half the ceiling lights and sat in an old armchair, across a coffee table from the two lovers. She fanned at the smoke in front of her face and said, "Hey, Wendy. Will. Got any more of that?"

Wendy sat upright on the couch, and Will fumbled for a pouch, mumbling something unintelligible. Wendy poured out marijuana on a paper, rolled it, licked the edge, pressed it shut, and twisted the ends, handing the joint across the table. Martha took a book of matches from a dirty ashtray, lit the joint, drew on it heavily, and held the smoke in her lungs, passing the joint back to Wendy. When she finally exhaled, she eased back in the armchair and said, "You didn't think I was coming back."

Wendy brushed stringy blond hair out of her eyes, passed the joint on to Will, and said, "No. Sonny's not with you?"

"Back at the mansion. He's with his mommy."

Wendy raised her eyebrows. "You two had a fight?"

Martha shrugged. "Not so much a fight as a surrender. His mother told me off, and he said I should take his car. I wanted to leave anyway."

"What's he doing?"

"Beats me."

"You going back out?"

"Not while she's there."

There was a knock at the door. Martha got up reluctantly and opened the door. There stood a young man in a blue Amish blouse, black vest, and heavy denim jacket. He held a black felt hat in his hands.

Martha said, "Oh, it's you." She turned around and walked back into the room.

The Amish man said, "A fellow let me in. Can we talk?" followed by something in Dutch dialect. Martha answered in kind, and waved him into the room.

6

Friday, November 1
8:20 P.M.

WHEN Arne Laughton, president of Millersburg College, entered
the front door of the Favor mansion, Daniel was waiting to take
his coat and galoshes. The two exchanged glances when they heard
Favor break out into laughter in the parlor next to the front foyer.
Daniel folded the tall president's long coat over his arm and said,
"If you don't mind, sir, Ms. Favor won't be but a minute."

Puzzled, Laughton looked in at the parlor door and saw Favor
seated on the divan with her back to him. He caught DiSalvo's
gaze and waved awkwardly to the lawyer. DiSalvo acknowledged
the president with a fractional tip of his head. In a far corner sat
Sonny Favor, fidgeting.

Laughton stepped back into the foyer. Daniel offered a straight-
backed chair, and the president sat with his slender hands on his
knees, listening to whatever brief snatches of conversation he could
understand. Intermittently, he made out key phrases, and, with
growing concern, he moved his chair closer to the parlor door. He
listened intently and ran his fingers occasionally through white hair.
By the time Favor came out to him, Laughton thought he had overheard the loss of a sizable portion of Millersburg College's long-
term funding.

"MY DEAR Mr. President," Favor said, and took Laughton's out-
stretched hand in both of hers. "I hope you haven't been waiting
long. It's business, you see, with Mr. DiSalvo."

She reached up and linked her arm in his, and with Sonny following, she guided the president into the bar, where she poured two drinks and toasted, "To Millersburg College!"

Laughton held his martini aloft and repeated the toast. He took a substantial swallow and said, "Forgive me, Juliet, if I show too much concern. Or if my concern is misplaced. But do I understand correctly that you're to reduce funding for our college next year?"

"Why, Arne. You've been listening at keyholes again."

Laughton blushed and stammered, "I'm sorry, but . . ."

With a dismissive wave of her hand, Favor said, "Arne, Arne. You can't expect the Favors to carry the college indefinitely."

A flush rose in Laughton's face, and he gulped the rest of his drink. Unsure what to say, he held out his glass, and Favor refilled it, smiling.

"Arne," Favor said, handing over the refill. "You didn't support me for chairwoman of the board of trustees last May."

"Juliet," Laughton began.

Favor interrupted. "Oh, come now, Arne. Surely we needn't worry about such little matters as these. As much as the Favors have been a friend to this institution? Not at all. But this can be repaired easily, Arne. There's the December meeting yet, and we can't operate too much longer with an interim chairman. He's not that good, anyway, don't you agree?"

"Juliet, I don't think . . . "

"Sure, Arne, sure. Now I do hope you'll stay for dinner. Nine o'clock in the formal dining room. And you're dressed just right." She stepped close to the president and played coyly with his tie, as if their relationship permitted her an extra measure of familiarity. "Always such a gentlemen."

Laughton straightened his tie. "I'm not sure, Juliet."

"I insist. Please. See Daniel. And we will talk some more after dinner."

"I hardly think this is the sort of thing to discuss over dessert," Laughton said gruffly.

"Such a tone!" Favor chided. "I won't sign any papers until to-morrow, anyway, so you needn't worry about your precious money. There's time yet, and we should use it. Don't you agree? Please, Arne. Stay just a bit longer and we'll sit down to a nice meal. Daniel is preparing sautéed Casco Bay sea scallops with peanuts and chives, plus Backaofa Alsace Style sea bass, or lamb with haricots à la Tourangelle. So how can you resist, Arne?"

"Perhaps, but I'm going to have to do something about my car."

"What's wrong out there?" Favor asked with indifference.

"Your Daniel has plowed a lane, but not much more than that. And in front of the house there are three cars, now, with little room for more. The drifts keep piling up, and I'm not sure any of us will be able to leave, if it keeps up out there."

"Is it any better around back?" Favor asked, cataloging in her mind the people yet to arrive. To Sonny she quipped, "At least we don't have your Lexus to worry about, do we?"

"Haven't been around back," Laughton said uneasily, watching the blood rise in Sonny Favor's cheeks.

"Can you please check with Daniel?" Favor asked Laughton, turning her back to Sonny.

Somewhat offended, Laughton replied, "Certainly, Juliet. If you wish."

"Thank you, Arne. And please tell Daniel to turn on the lights all around the house. I'd like him to plow again, too, this time wider. Yours is not the last car that has to get up my drive tonight."

JULIET led Sonny back to the parlor, where they found Sally Favor and Jenny snuggled up to either side of a blushing Henry DiSalvo on the divan.

Favor erupted, "Oh, for God's sake, Sally!"

"Mother dear," Sally said, obviously still drunk. She hugged DiSalvo as if he were a fuzzy bear.

"I had hoped you'd left," Favor said coldly.

"Can't get down the drive, Mommy. Guess we'll stay for dinner."

"You'll do no such thing!"

"You see that, Sonny?" Sally drawled. "Mommy's true colors."

"Why do you always have to push it, Sally?" Sonny complained.

"Because you won't stand up to her!" Sally shot back. "You're pathetic, Sonny. Stand up to her."

Sally bounded suddenly to her feet, took Sonny by the arms and pulled him into the center of the room. "Stand up to her just once, Sonny."

"You're drunk," Sonny observed disapprovingly.

"So what?"

"I don't see why you have to be so rude to everyone," Sonny complained.

"Just to her, Sonny. Do you really think you can keep your trust?"

"Just three more years."

"What do you mean? Didn't you hear her lawyer?"

"You were listening?"

"Oh, for God's sake, Sonny! Grow up."

Sonny shook his head and retreated to the fireplace, where he sullenly tapped the smooth brass rugby trophy on the mantel. Enraged, Sally closed the distance to him quickly, seized the trophy in both hands, and threw it onto the plush carpet in the direction of her mother. It gave a loud thunk and rolled a foot or so to her mother's feet.

Mrs. Favor launched herself at Sally, grabbed her by the neck, and twisted. In the brief scuffle that ensued, their legs became entangled, and they spun and fell to the floor as if spite and rejection had conspired to stir a vortex that dragged them down.

Stepping forward, Sonny managed to separate the two stunned women without getting kicked, while DiSalvo, embarrassed, returned the trophy to the mantel. Jenny sat quietly on the divan, smiling as if in victory. Nervously, DiSalvo centered the trophy on the mantel.

Struggling to her feet, Sally sputtered, "You Absolute Bitch!"

Juliet straightened her skirt and blazer and tried to refasten her carnation. Frustrated, she tore the flower off and threw it into the fire.

"Really, folks," DiSalvo said and shook his head.

"I know, Henry. I apologize," Juliet offered, and glanced angrily at her daughter.

Sally rubbed at her throat, looked woefully at Jenny, walked over to take her lover's hand, and stood her up in front of the divan. To Sonny, Sally rasped, "If you don't break free from her, you'll never have a life, Sonny. Money isn't that important."

Pausing, she looked in turn at Sonny, at her mother, and at DiSalvo. Softly she said, "Money isn't really anything at all," and escorted Jenny from the room.

PHILLIPS Royce, chairman of the art department at Millersburg College, turned up the drive to Favor Manor behind Daniel's small tractor. He followed slowly in the track the plow cleared and came up to the oval in front of the house, wiper blades snapping at the snow and ice. Instead of parking in front, where there were several other cars angled into a snowbank, Royce followed Daniel's plow back around the east side of the house to the north, and parked in the rear. He stepped out into the blizzard, huddled next to the car, fought the wind to close the door, and sprinted to one of the back doors.

Inside, the art professor stomped his boots without closing the door tightly, and this brought loud complaints from the three cooks working in the spacious kitchen to his left. He turned back to close the door, but Daniel pushed in behind him. The butler closed the door with effort and caught a stern look from one of the cooks, who reached up to steady several pans and skillets that had started banging in the draft from the open door. Bliss left his long black dress coat on and helped Royce out of his coat. He took a whisk-broom hanging on the doorknob and knelt to brush snow from the professor's pants and boots.

Phillips Royce was a small man of fifty-nine, not much taller than

Juliet Favor. He pulled off a knit skullcap to reveal a large, clean-shaven head. He had big eyes and wore thick, black-rimmed glasses. His black mustache was full and long, covering most of his upper lip and twisting out into fancy, waxed curls on either end. He was dressed in a brown corduroy suit, with worn leather patches at the elbows. He twisted the ends of his mustache carefully, thanked Daniel, and ascended the stairs at the rear of the house without further comment.

The staircase led to a vestibule at the back of the house on the second floor, where there were doors to two bedrooms separated by a long hall. He went directly to the west bedroom and halted before opening the door. Inside, he heard the playful voices of two young, drunk women. At the door to the east bedroom he heard nothing. He turned back, passed down the middle hall, and came out at the top landing of the front staircase. Here was another hall, perpendicular to the first, giving access to the master bedroom. At the west end of this hall, he stopped to listen again to the women's voices, now on his right, and then entered a door on his left, to the master bedroom. Sitting on the edge of the bed, he removed his old boots, fluffed two big pillows, and lay back against the head of the bed.

In a few minutes, Juliet came in from the master bath. She took off her blazer and threw it on the foot of the bed. With her blue skirt hitched above her knees, she climbed onto the bed and moved on hands and knees to Royce. With several pillows, she propped herself on her left side to face him, and slipped her hand under his belt buckle.

7

Friday, November 1
9:00 P.M.

ON THE front steps of Martha's dorm, her Amish friend, John Schlabaugh, said, "That boy's not treating you right, and you'd better believe it."

Martha stood shivering with the door propped open and said, "How many really nice things do you have, John? What's wrong with wanting nice things?"

"You shouldn't be smoking that silly weed," John said. He buttoned his denim jacket, turned up his collar, and put on his black hat.

Martha let the door close a little and took a step back.

"When can I see you?" John asked.

"You don't approve of me," Martha said matter-of-factly.

"You know how I feel about you, Martha," John complained. "Always have, and you know it."

"You saved my life once," Martha said. "I'm grateful, really I am. But that doesn't mean we're going out."

Schlabaugh drew gloves out of his hip pocket, put them on, and slapped his palms together. He tipped his hat and said, "I'm not giving up."

8

Friday, November 1
9:20 P.M.

IN A PEACH and rose evening gown, Juliet Favor descended the grand staircase to the foyer and was greeted enthusiastically by several guests holding drinks. She tarried among them, enjoying their attentions, as she inquired about each professor or administrator. On passing through the parlor, she picked up several more people in her train and moved casually, chatting amiably, into the spacious dining room. There, a large oval table was set for dinner. Daniel stood formally, immaculate in his tuxedo. With him were six Amish children, hired as servers for the evening. The children were dressed in plain Amish garb, denim trousers and vests for the boys, and matching dark plum dresses with white aprons and prayer caps for the girls. They were "pin" Amish, from an Old Order sect that eschewed buttons, fastening their clothes with straight pins. They lived on a farm adjoining the Favor property, across the road from a family of "Knopfer," or button Amish, who held neither conversation nor fellowship with their backward neighbors.

At Daniel's signal, the children took up positions evenly spaced around the oval table. Favor stood at the middle of the table, with her back to a large bay window. Floodlights outside reflected off the snow and cast a white, high-key light into the room.

The president, dean, and their faculty, almost all of them chairpersons of an academic department or program, found their seats by consulting place cards on the dinner plates. When Juliet sat, they all sat.

With her back to the west, Juliet had Daniel behind her, standing before serving tables that lined the long curve of the bay window. Harry Favor had added the window and its built-in tables when he enlarged the room some years ago so that Juliet could entertain on a grand scale. The food was laid out in chafing dishes on these tables. As the servers finished pouring wine and water, Favor lifted her glass to make a toast. The guests lifted their glasses with her.

"To a new era at Millersburg College," Favor proclaimed. "To new things and new ways."

Around the table, the guests collectively made their responses, some enthusiastically, others murmuring. As President Laughton rose to make a toast, Favor signaled for him to take his seat. He missed her signal and started to talk, at which point Favor said, "Arne, please. Let's save that sort of thing for later." Red-faced, the president sat down.

Annoyed, Favor cut short her remarks and brought business to the fore. "You will each find," she said, "an envelope at your plate. These are my responses to your various funding proposals to the Harry Favor Trust Foundation. Some of you will be pleased, but, I'm afraid, in most cases, we've had to make significant cutbacks. You each have an appointment slip for tomorrow, when we can negotiate your cases individually."

Favor stopped and watched as most of the guests at the table began to open their envelopes. She saw that only Michael Branden and Dean William Coffee refrained, and smiled.

"Please," Favor said. "You can read those later. For the moment, Daniel has prepared an excellent meal. Please indicate your choice of entrée to the waiter assigned to you."

While three of the children served the first course, the other three circulated to take orders. Favor sat quietly for the most part during the meal. The several questions put to her about budgets she deflected adroitly, keeping the conversation light. On her side of the oval, to her immediate left sat Sonny Favor, who said nothing during the meal. On Favor's right sat Dean of the Faculty William Blake Coffee, in his position long enough to know better than to discuss business with Juliet Favor over dinner. Next to Coffee, around the table to Favor's right was Henry DiSalvo. At the right end of the oval sat Kathryn Aimsworthy, chairwoman of the sociology department and the anthropology program. Opposite her, at the far end of the oval, there was Walt Camry, chairman of the English department. To his right sat President Laughton, who was on Sonny's left. Facing Juliet Favor from left to right on the other side of the oval sat Dick Pomeroy, chairman of the chemistry department; Michael Branden, history chairman and founder of the Millersburg College Museum of Battlefield Firearms; Phillips Royce directly opposite Favor; Carol Jenkins, chairwoman of economics; Elizabeth Williamson, women's studies chairwoman; and to Aimsworthy's right, Rebecca Willhite, physical education director. In all, then, twelve guests sat at the table with Juliet and Sonny Favor.

Food was served from the tables lining the curve of the large bay window. Light came from several candlesticks and from the window, reflected from the snowfall. Polite discussions in genteel voices were the rule. Juliet gradually withdrew from the conversation, the back of her neck and head giving her obvious discomfort. By the end of the meal, most guests knew to take their envelopes, make a graceful exit, and go home to read in private of their department's fate.

Among the last to leave was President Laughton, who was politely rebuffed. Phillips Royce, who intended to stay, was also refused. As Daniel saw him out the back door, Favor went up the rear staircase holding the back of her head. Soon after that, the Amish servers finished clearing the tables, and they left together to walk home in the snow. And by 11:30 P.M., Daniel Bliss had dismissed the kitchen staff, plowed one more time, and retired to his quarters at the back of the property, in a ranch-style home behind a four-bay garage.

9

CAROLINE Branden was out with the sunrise, bundled head to toe against the cold, filling her backyard birdfeeders. At the back of the lot, near sheer cliffs overlooking a wide Amish valley blanketed in white, she filled two finch feeder tubes with black thistle seed. At several stations in the middle of the yard, she put out whole sunflower seed and cracked corn. On a pole near the kitchen window, she tied on a new strip of raw suet and replaced a cake of commercial peanut suet in a square wire cage. Pulling her bags of seed and other supplies on a green plastic toboggan with yellow rope, she trudged through the deep, soft snow to the door at the side of their full-length back porch. One at a time, she lifted the heavy bags up the steps, and stacked them inside, with the rest of her winter stores.

She brushed off snow and stomped her feet before crossing the length of the porch to a sliding door. There, she stepped into the Brandens' family room, slipped out of her yellow-and-black hooded ski parka, and sat on the couch to unlace her high snow boots. Black snow pants came off last, and she laid the whole outfit out on the carpet to dry. Down to blue jeans and a sweatshirt, she put on fluffy green slippers and found her husband, Professor Michael Branden, in the kitchen, still in his blue cotton pajamas. He had a mug of freshly made coffee waiting for her at the kitchen table.

Caroline Branden was a tall, slender woman with long, light-auburn hair. Her husband, equally trim, was half a head shorter, with brown hair graying at the sides.

"No self-respecting bird is going to be out in this weather," Branden remarked as his wife sat down opposite him at the large maple table, the gift of an Amish friend.

"Six kisses says you're wrong, Michael," she said confidently, sipping her coffee.

"I'll take that bet," Branden replied and smiled. "Get bigger feeders and you wouldn't have to go out every morning."

The phone rang, and he got up slowly to answer it, as Caroline remarked, "I like things just the way they are."

As he spoke on the phone, Caroline watched her first customer arrive, a male downy woodpecker, with his black and white coat and a small patch of red at the back of his head.

Branden motioned her to the phone and whispered, "It's Evelyn Carson."

Caroline queried him with her eyes as she came up beside him, and he cupped the receiver and said, "Martha Lehman" as he handed her the phone.

Caroline took the phone, and the professor remained at her side. She said hello, listened, and said, "My God, Evelyn. Have you got her there? Not at the hospital?"

Then Branden heard her say, at intervals, "Of course. You're sure she's not bleeding? Why not? OK, keep her there with you. Of course. No. I'm coming down."

Caroline hung up the phone and headed directly for her boots in the family room. As she sat on the edge of the couch to lace them up, she said, "Martha's over at Evelyn's office. She's got blood on her apron. And it's not fresh blood, Michael. I mean, it's . . . I don't know. Evelyn says she's not bleeding. And there's a Lexus with its front end smashed in, parked in the alley. Does Martha have a car?"

"No," the professor replied, "but her boyfriend has a Lexus."

"I'm going down to Evelyn's office." Caroline said.

"I'll go with you," Branden said.

"No. Better idea would be to call down to the sheriff's office first and see if anything's been put out on the radios about a car crash. Some kind of accident."

"Take your cell phone," he said, and turned back to the kitchen.

PAST a silent and deserted courthouse square, Caroline Branden turned right on the Wooster road, and drove north through plowed slush to a pink Victorian house south of Joel Pomerene Hospital. Here, several large Victorian homes on the left side of the road had been renovated to hold offices for doctors, lawyers, and other professionals. In an alley beside the pink house, Caroline pulled her Miata to a stop in deep snow, wedging the front of the sports car into a snowbank, next to a silver Lexus with its front end smashed into a light pole. Caroline got out of her car, brushed snow from the driver's-side window of the Lexus, and saw a deflated airbag hanging from the steering wheel. She followed tracks through the snow to a side door, climbed the stairs to the second floor, pushed in through one of the heavy office doors, and found Martha Lehman sitting on a couch beside Evelyn Carson.

Pulling off her coat, Caroline sat in a recliner near the couch. Martha turned her head toward her old friend, but her eyes registered no reaction.

Evelyn Carson eased Martha Lehman back from the edge of the couch and let go of her hand. She motioned for Caroline to follow her to a small office bathroom, where she washed blood from her hands.

Taking a seat at a desk in a far corner of the office, Dr. Carson said, "I found her curled up outside my door there, when I got in around 7:00. She's not hurt. The blood's only on her apron, plus her hands and whatever she's touched. At first I couldn't get her to move. Once I did get her inside, she wouldn't talk."

Caroline asked, "Won't talk or can't talk?"

"This is trauma," Evelyn said, "so it doesn't matter right now whether it's 'won't' or 'can't.' She's mute again, just like before."

"You got her through this once, Evelyn. She'll pull through again," Caroline said.

The phone rang and Evelyn answered it and handed the receiver to Caroline, saying, "It's Mike."

Caroline took the phone and said, "It's not good, Michael."

"It may be worse than you think," the professor replied.

"You talked to the dispatchers?"

"Juliet Favor has been murdered," he said flatly, "and an inebriated Sally Favor is being questioned at the scene."

10

Saturday, November 2
8:00 A.M.

MIKE Branden climbed the snow-covered front steps at the Favor home early Saturday morning in bright sun, and heard Sheriff Bruce Robertson's booming voice inside. Under different circumstances, the professor would have smiled, familiar as he was with Holmes County's colorful lawman. The professor had not seen Robertson since late in August, when Branden's involvement with the sheriff's office typically diminished with the start of the fall semester at Millersburg College.

The preceding summer had been a peaceful one, a year since Robertson had nearly died in a fire at a roadside accident. Robertson's long recuperation from the burns and subsequent infections had forced a hiatus, and, in the year and a half that he was out, the operation of the small-town sheriff's office had been in the hands of Administrative Captain Bobby Newell and Chief Deputy Kessler. Several promotions had taken place, most notably Lieutenant Dan Wilsher to Patrol Captain, and the odd corporal here and there to sergeant. By the time Professor Branden had taken chalk in hand for the fall term at Millersburg College, Robertson had assumed full-time command again, keeping the peace among the many Amish and Mennonite sects of rural Holmes County, Ohio.

By Branden's reckoning, in the year and a half since their last major case together, there had been, in all of Holmes County, only five assaults and twenty-two burglaries or thefts, a crime rate typical of a single day in Cleveland, some seventy miles to the north. Ominous, then, Branden thought in the cold morning light, that murder had once again found sleepy Millersburg. Even more so that it had invaded the repose of one of Ohio's several dozen small colleges.

Branden crossed through heavily tracked snow on the front porch, took off his gloves, and pushed the front doorbell. As Sergeant Ricky Niell opened the heavy wood and glass door to him, Branden slid back the hood of his winter coat and stepped into the large foyer of the house.

Ricky Niell was dressed in a neatly pressed brown and black uniform, his black hair and thin mustache trimmed fastidiously.

Sheriff Robertson stood opposite the front door, at the top of the grand staircase, in a gray suit, with his red tie loosened over a white shirt whose collar seemed a size too small. He bellowed, "Mike, wait there!" and started down the staircase, careful to side-step yellow plastic number markers that had been laid in several places on the beige carpet.

Branden turned to Niell, offered his hand, and said, "Congratulations, Ricky."

Niell fingered the sergeant's stripes on his left sleeve and said, "Thanks."

Branden eyed the insignia and said, "Well, yes. That too, but I meant on your marriage to Ellie Troyer."

Niell nodded and smiled. He looked down at his shoes, and again said, "Thanks."

"You're going to hear from Caroline about this," Branden teased.

Ricky watched the sheriff descend the last few steps and said, "We eloped. Thought that was best."

"Yeah, I know," the professor said, "but that didn't give anyone a chance to throw Ellie a shower."

Niell shifted his weight nervously.

Branden said, "You got out of the wedding, but now you're

going to have to sit through a couple of wedding showers. You and all those women. It might have been better to have had a nice little wedding and get it all over with at once."

Niell chuckled and said, "She's worth it, Doc."

Robertson crossed the entryway to them and asked, "Who's worth it?" He hitched his pants up awkwardly and pulled on the front of his ill-fitting suit coat to align it as best he could.

"You've put on some weight, Bruce," Branden observed dryly.

"It's nothing," Robertson said, sounding annoyed. "Who's worth it?" he repeated.

"Ellie Troyer-Niell," Branden answered.

"Don't I know it!" Robertson blustered. "She's got me broke in about where I like it." He pointed to Niell's sleeve and added, "Did you see these sergeant's stripes, Mike?"

"Yes," Branden murmured, distracted. He moved away from the front door to look at an area that had been marked off with crime scene tape on the black marble floor. Eric Shetler, Robertson's photographer, was kneeling there, taking low-angle photos of the small area.

"Some significance here?" Branden asked, looking back at Robertson.

"That's gonna be where Juliet Favor died," the sheriff said. "There was a fight here, and you can see where she cracked her head on the floor. Then, someone carried her up the stairs, there, and there are blood drops on the carpet, leading up to her bedroom."

Staying outside the tape, Branden got down on his hands and knees and studied a small star crack in the black floor. If it hadn't been marked, he would not have seen it. He got back on his feet, took off his heavy coat, and draped it over an upholstered chair in the corner of the large entryway. "What else do you have?" he asked.

Robertson led the way up the stairs to the hallway outside Juliet Favor's bedroom. Looking in, Branden saw Coroner Missy Taggert and two lab technicians bent over Favor's body, studying a small patch of blood at the back of her skull. Favor was lying on her side, head on a pillow, as if she had simply fallen asleep there. The covers were pulled up over her shoulders.

Back downstairs, in the front foyer with Ricky Niell, Branden asked, "Have you talked with any witnesses, people who came out, that sort of thing?"

"We've just started," Robertson said and frowned. He turned to Niell and quietly said, "Niell, put one of your deputies on each of the doors. Nobody gets upstairs except us, got it?"

Niell nodded, "Yes, sir."

On reflection, Robertson added, "Look, Ricky, this one's going to be a mess. There'll be a regular stampede out here once word gets around. Anyone who insists on staying, you send around to the kitchen door in back. Have Armbruster take them all into the dining room from there. They can each wait there until we get statements. I'll want to know what they're doing here this morning. Why they came out. And whether they were here last night. How many's that going to be, Doc?"

"Probably a dozen at dinner. Kitchen staff makes for more."

"Get a list started, Ricky," Robertson said. "We're gonna do this one by the book."

"I've got one for the staff already," Niell said. He took a spiral notebook out of a creased uniform breast pocket. "The butler already gave me the staff on duty last night."

"OK. Good," Robertson said. "Let's get Armbruster started making a list like that for this morning. The whole campus will probably be out here before the day's over."

Robertson said to Branden, "You'll be an asset on this case, Mike, with so many college people involved. Without you, we'd need a program and a scorecard to keep all the players straight."

"You might consider me a suspect, Bruce."

"Get real, Doc."

"Hey, I was out here last night like everyone else."

"I'll kick you off the case as soon as you screw up. But maybe you don't like the idea of working a case during the school year."

"Doesn't bother me."

"OK, then. I can use your help on this one."

"I hoped you'd say that," Branden said.

"Then how's about you and I go interview the butler?" Robertson asked. He glanced back to Niell for a name.

Niell flipped a page in his notebook and said, "Daniel Bliss."

BLISS was seated at his small desk, wearing a trim blue blazer and matching bow tie over a white shirt. He made a show of rising slowly to greet the sheriff and the professor.

"Daniel Bliss, butler to the Favors," he said formally. "Sheriff, I see no reason for your captain to have detained young Miss Sally, much less to have subjected her to a grueling interrogation."

"Actually," said the sheriff, "there is good reason to question Sally Favor, Mr. Bliss."

"She has admitted to spending the night, nothing more."

"We haven't detained her yet," Robertson said. "Not officially. We're really just waiting for her to sober up, as I understand it."

"I've told your captain that Sally will say nothing more until the family lawyer arrives."

Robertson changed the subject. "I understand there were quite a few people out here last night."

"I've already given your sergeant a list of the staff."

"I'll need a list of the guests, too," Robertson said.

Bliss turned to his desk, took a handwritten list from the blotter, and gave it to Robertson. "This is the invitation list. I've been working on it for you just now. So far as I remember, everyone attended. Perhaps Professor Branden could verify the list."

Robertson handed the list to Branden without looking at it.

Captain Bobby Newell entered the narrow room from a door to the kitchen and said, "Lawyer's here."

Newell was dressed in gray sweats, as if he'd been summoned to the scene from the gym. He was stocky and well muscled. His habit of flexing the muscles in his massive arms and shoulders made him seem constantly agitated.

Branden asked him, "Didn't get much from Sally?"

"No," Newell said. "She's still pretty wasted. Her girlfriend up in the back bedroom is the same. They say her mother was drunk last night, too."

"That's not possible," Daniel countered.

Newell ignored the butler. "I've collected several champagne bottles out of Sally Favor's room and elsewhere, and enough gin was served here, last night, to keep ten people drunk," he told Robertson. "Gave all the bottles to Dr. Taggert already."

"You've no right to search through people's rooms," Daniel complained.

"Oh, I very much do, sir," Newell answered. "At any rate, the young lady is still inebriated. It's going to be a while before we get anything coherent out of her."

Robertson tapped the list Branden held and said, "Now, Mr. Bliss. For the record, do you consider that anyone on your list there will have had a motive for murder?"

Branden was surprised by the direct question, and from what he saw in the butler's expression, so was Bliss. Newell instinctively moved a little closer and sat on the edge of Bliss's desk, crowding the butler somewhat. Robertson held Bliss's eyes and waited.

Bliss sighed as if his integrity had been impeached by imbeciles, and said, "Any of them."

"And why do you say that?" Robertson asked.

"They all were taking cutbacks in their budgets."

"Hardly seems a reason to kill someone," Robertson said.

"There were to be wholesale changes in the disposition of the Favor estate. Mr. Henry DiSalvo was to come out here today to help Ms. Favor meet with each department head from last night's banquet. There was to be another banquet tonight, with the rest of the academic department heads, and meetings with them on Sunday. Everything was going to be changed, even the children's trusts."

"I see President Laughton's name is on your list. Do you consider him a suspect, too?" Robertson asked.

"He had more reason than most," Bliss replied flatly.

Robertson stared wordlessly at Bliss, waiting for an explanation.

Said Bliss, "The college budget, as a whole, was to be reduced, and he and Ms. Favor had had a disagreement over leadership of the college board."

Robertson eyed the butler for a long thirty seconds and said, "Thank you, Daniel. That'll be all for now. I want you to stay in your room here for the next several hours."

Bliss blanched indignantly. "That will be quite impossible."

The sheriff stepped eyeball-to-eyeball with the butler and raised his voice to say, "Stay here, Bliss. Talk to no one. Am I understood?"

Daniel sputtered a few syllables and backed up against the edge of his desk, displacing Bobby Newell.

Robertson said, "Captain Newell will take your statement now."

Newell nodded and took a notepad out of his waistband.

Robertson asked him, "Sally Favor?" and Newell pointed toward the kitchen door.

BRANDEN followed the burly sheriff through the swinging door, and the two found Sally in a white terrycloth bathrobe, her short hair disheveled, hovering over a cup of coffee at a small round table in the corner of the large kitchen. Henry DiSalvo sat next to her in an old-fashioned three-piece suit. His long winter coat was draped over his knees.

As soon as he saw Robertson, DiSalvo rose to his feet, laid his coat over the back of his chair, and said, "Miss Favor is not answering any more questions, Bruce."

"You're an estate lawyer, Henry," Robertson said. "Sally, from what I've seen upstairs, you're gonna need a criminal lawyer. I'd be happy to recommend someone."

"I'm sure you would," Sally muttered, cradling her head. She took a slow drink of her coffee and said, "Henry has been our family's lawyer for twenty years. Besides, I don't need a trial lawyer. Didn't kill my mother, you see."

"Don't say anything," DiSalvo said.

Robertson sat next to Sally at the table and said, "I understand you didn't get along very well with your mother."

"Don't respond to that," DiSalvo said.

Robertson, impatient, shot back, "We've already got that from her brother!"

"She's not going to tell you anything more today."

"My mother was a high-society phony," Sally said, rubbing her temples.

"That's enough," DiSalvo said forcefully. "Sheriff Robertson, you do not have my permission to question my client further."

"We're going to talk to her, Henry," Robertson said calmly.

Branden offered, "Sally's a former student of mine, Bruce. Perhaps she could come down to your office later today."

Robertson looked pensively at Branden, seemed to smile, and then said to Sally, "Would that be all right with you?"

Sally whispered, "Whatever Henry says."

To DiSalvo, Robertson said, "If she's innocent, it'd be better for her to tell us what she knows."

DiSalvo said, "I'll let you know, Bruce. Maybe sometime Monday."

"It has got to be today," Robertson countered. "Preferably this morning."

"We'll see," DiSalvo said.

Robertson glared at the lawyer, and then turned to Sally. "I'll see you down at the jail, later this morning, Miss Favor. Don't forget," he added, and stood up. "Better yet, we'll all go in together."

"It's Saturday," Sally complained.

Robertson didn't answer her. Pouting, she got up and headed for the stairs to the second floor.

"No, you don't, young lady," Robertson said.

"I need to change," Sally said wearily.

"You sit here and drink coffee," Robertson said. "I've got a lot of house to go through, and I'll let you know when you can get back up to your bedroom."

"Just what do you expect me to do for clothes, Sheriff?"

"Your room is being used to question Jenny Radcliffe."

"Jenny had nothing to do with this," Sally said.

"Then you won't mind if I talk with her next," Robertson countered.

BEFORE the interview with Jenny Radcliffe, Professor Branden stepped into the pantry adjoining the kitchen and used his cell phone to call Evelyn Carson's office. He inquired first about Martha Lehman, learned there had been little change, and then said, "Call Cal Troyer, Caroline. She's been attending his church lately."

"Let me try to ask her about that," Caroline said, and muted the phone. Back on, she said, "I still get no reaction, Michael."

Branden frowned and scratched nervously at the back of his head. "I still don't know what we've got out here at the Favors' place. Isn't she talking at all?"

"She's come around some. Recognizes where she is, I think, but she is definitely not talking."

"Does she nod her head? Anything like that?"

"She just stares at Evelyn. Tracks her with her eyes, wherever she goes."

11

Saturday, November 2
8:35 A.M.

BRANDEN followed Robertson up the rear staircase to the second-floor vestibule at the back of the house. At the west end, Robertson turned left and opened a door to Sally Favor's bedroom. Inside, Branden and Robertson found Jenny Radcliffe seated on the edge of a four-poster bed, wearing blue silk pajamas, and wrapped at the waist in an ornate Amish comforter. Daniel Bliss stood beside her, offering coffee on a silver tray with a delicate porcelain creamer and sugar jar. Bliss looked sideways at the sheriff, and stayed bent at the waist, while Jenny lifted a cup and saucer with trembling fingers. When he straightened up, Bliss said, "Don't worry. I'm going back downstairs now, Sheriff."

A deputy had been standing inside the door, and to him Robertson said, "Deputy, escort Mr. Bliss to the kitchen, and see that he stays there."

Daniel left with an unflustered slowness, the deputy following.

Robertson took to pacing a small circle on the carpet in front of Jenny's bed and signaled with a sweep of his eyes that Branden should have a look around the room. Without touching anything, Branden studied a low vanity strewn with champagne bottles and cigarette butts in several ashtrays. He pointed out two small, blackened pipes to Robertson and then opened a door opposite to the one they had entered. This let out into a hallway, and directly across was an opened door to the master bedroom. Branden nodded across the hall to Coroner Melissa Taggert, who was bent over at the head of the bed, examining the back of Juliet Favor's skull. Branden saw blond hair matted with blood and a pale death face.

Robertson pulled up a small metal makeup chair from the vanity, turned it backward in front of Jenny, and straddled it. He watched her blow on her coffee and asked, "What can you tell me about last night?"

Radcliffe said nothing. She brushed curly brown hair out of her eyes and sipped coffee, gazing morosely down.

"There must have been a lot of blood, Jenny," Robertson said. "We're gonna find out how you two cleaned it all up."

Nothing from Radcliffe.

"You did a poor job of it, anyways," Robertson continued. "There were obvious signs of blood when we tested the foyer floor. You've surely gotten some of it on you, too. We can type-test and get a DNA profile from even the slightest trace. They call that the Polymerase Chain Reaction, or the PCR. Now I couldn't tell you for a minute what that means, but if you left even the minutest trace, we've got you. Both of you."

Jenny looked contemptuously at Robertson and then stared at the cup and saucer resting in her lap.

"How did you get her upstairs?" Robertson pressed, a little more sternly. "There's a blood trail up the steps and into the master bedroom."

A vacant stare from Radcliffe.

Slowly, Robertson got up from the chair. Reaching around to his hip pocket, he took out a wad of little plastic evidence bags, and at the vanity, he scooped the two pipes into one of them. Back in front of Jenny Radcliffe, he held up the pipes and said, "Get dressed. You're going into town."

When Branden joined him out in the back hall, the sheriff whispered, "Sonny Favor has already told us that Sally and her mom had a catfight on the parlor carpet last night because Sally is a lesbian. The way Favor's head is cracked open, looks like they had another one later, on or near the grand staircase. That leaves hauling her back up to bed and cleaning up the foyer floor."

"You're checking for blood in the sinks, and bloody rags? That sort of thing?" Branden asked.

"Yep. Clothes and such in the house, and all over the grounds outside."

"You haven't gotten anything from either Jenny or Sally yet?"

"Just like what you heard, Mike. But it's Sonny who's been talking. A regular little gabber, that one, so far. I can pretty much tell you everything that happened here last night, and the butler's right. A good twenty people have motive. But the girls are lesbians, and Juliet Favor spat acid over that last night, from what Sonny has said."

"At best, Bruce, Sonny Favor is a confused and frightened kid," Branden said. "I ought to know, since I'm his academic adviser. Whatever you're getting from him will be shaky."

"He's just a freshman. How you gonna know a kid that well, this soon?"

"He's in my seminar class."

"Great! Liberal indoctrination! You guys don't trust kids to do college work until they've had your propaganda course."

"You know very well that the purpose of the Freshman Readings is to help get them adjusted to college-level expectations, while letting at least one professor get to know them well as their adviser."

"Whatever you say, Mike, but damn. I've read your list of Freshman Readings topics, and you guys gotta be somewhere left of Mao or something."

"Not everyone, Bruce," Branden said.

"OK, what's your topic?"

"The Real Causes of the American Civil War."

Robertson rolled his eyes.

"Look, Bruce. I just try to get the students thinking from each of the various perspectives. So they'll realize that historical events are subject to many interpretations."

"Why? It was slavery that caused the Civil War."

"It helps them become better thinkers."

"Whatever."

"Look, Bruce. It's really Sonny we're talking about, and I can tell you that whatever he's saying this morning, he doesn't yet really understand what has happened."

"You'll have to let me be the judge of that."

"Let me talk with him, Bruce."

Robertson studied the professor's face intently. Frowning, he motioned for Branden to stay put. At the east end of the hall, he poked his head into Sonny Favor's bedroom and spoke a few sentences to someone inside. Soon, a deputy came out with Captain Dan Wilsher, and the three men whispered at the end of the hall for several minutes. Occasionally, one of them glanced back down the hall at Branden. Wilsher and the deputy then went down the rear staircase, and Robertson motioned Branden into Sonny Favor's room.

12

Saturday, November 2
8:50 A.M.

BRANDEN entered Sonny Favor's room ahead of the sheriff and found the boy seated at a computer desk, playing with a flight simulator. Robertson stepped in behind Branden, closed the door, and leaned back against it.

"I think we should talk, Sonny," Branden said.

Sonny looked back at Branden and returned to his game. Branden watched with growing annoyance as the plane on the screen rocketed up. Sonny rolled the plane over, nosed it down, and let go of the joystick, ignoring the warnings about an imminent crash. The plane hit the ground and exploded, and Sonny sat for a long time with his back to Branden, watching the fireball on the screen. When he stood up, he went straight to a wooden box at the foot of his bed, took out a baseball and glove, and repeatedly snapped the ball into the pocket of the glove, saying, "They shouldn't leave her bloody like that. When are they going to clean her up?"

Branden shrugged and watched the ball.

Sonny faced the wall next to the door, where Robertson had leaned casually back, and bounced the baseball onto the hardwood floor, against the wall, and back into his glove. He repeated this half a dozen times and then drew back and hurled the ball at Robertson's head.

Robertson ducked the missile, and it bounced back and crashed into a plastic model airplane on a shelf on the other side of the bed.

"Not a good idea, Sonny!" Branden shot.

"I want out of this house!" Sonny shouted.

"Is he under arrest?" Branden asked Robertson.

"No."

"Is there any reason he can't leave?"

"I still need to talk to him," Robertson said, eyes fixed on Sonny.

"I don't want to talk anymore," Sonny barked. "I've done nothing but talk all morning."

"I have one or two questions yet," Robertson said with forced restraint.

Sonny flopped back onto his bed and waved his arms in the air. "God, what is it?"

Robertson came forward into the bedroom and took off his suit coat. He folded it carefully and laid it over the back of a reading chair. He walked around the foot of the bed, found the baseball in a corner and dropped it into the glove on Sonny's left hand. Around on the other side of the bed, the sheriff took a position standing next to the professor, and asked, "When you phoned 911 this morning, Sonny, who else was in the house?"

"I don't know."

"Was Bliss here?"

"I used the intercom to try to reach him. No. He didn't answer."

"Your sister?"

"I suppose so."

"You didn't check?"

"No."

"Any particular reason?"

"What do you care?"

"You found your mother dead and didn't check around for your sister?"

"I don't like her Jenny."

"You shared that sentiment with your mother, I understand."

"I told all that to the officer."

"He's a captain."

"If you say so."

"Did you hear anything last night?"

"I take a pill."

"But did you hear anything in the night?"

"I take sleeping pills and don't wake up until five or six."

"You didn't call until 6:30."

"I get headaches."

"You get headaches, or you wake up with headaches?"

"Wake up with them. Usually by five."

"How did you find your mother?"

"I don't want to talk about that."

"You're in the habit of wandering into her bedroom at five in the morning?"

Sonny didn't reply.

"Where did you find her?" Robertson pressed.

"I don't know."

"Sure you do."

"In bed, I guess. She was dead."

"How did you know she was dead?"

"I don't remember."

"Did you touch her?"

"God, no."

"Then how did you know?"

"I watched her, I guess."

"You stood and watched her? How long?"

"A while. I don't know. I kind of blacked out."

"Did you go anywhere else before you called?"

"No."

"You used the phone in the master bedroom?"

"Yes."

"Then it'd be a good half-hour that you 'watched her,' based on when you called. Could easily have been longer. Were you up by five, or was it six?"

"I don't know."

"Sure you do."

"I just found her, all right!"

"And you just stood there and watched her for half an hour, maybe more."

"Sure. Maybe. I don't know for sure."

"Did you touch anything besides the phone?"

"No."

"OK. That's enough for now," Robertson concluded after a long silence. "I'll want you to come down to my office later this morning. We'll all go in together."

Robertson thought further and asked, "Did you kids have another party here? Last night, after your mother went to bed?"

"No. I told you. I took a pill and went to bed."

"OK," Robertson said. "Be ready later this morning."

Sonny closed his eyes and pinched the bridge of his nose.

"I'm going to leave you with Professor Branden," Robertson added.

"OK, sure," Sonny said, rubbing his eyes.

Robertson retrieved his suit coat and pulled Branden out into the hall. Quietly he said, "He doesn't seem too traumatized."

"He's tired, Bruce. Probably also in shock."

"Does he seem normal to you? Kind of passive and frustrated too?"

"Sonny's not very assertive under the best of circumstances. And he's easily frustrated. He's been under enormous pressure from his mother for grades that are, frankly, beyond his capabilities," Branden said. "I see a lot of kids like that, lately. Let me talk with him a bit."

Robertson pulled the curtains open on a hallway window, and bright light reflected in off the snow. He shaded his eyes and gazed down at the parking lot behind the house. "I've probably got a dozen people to talk to," he said.

Branden looked down and counted seven vehicles parked at various angles against the snow Daniel had banked with his plow.

"Do you need me to come down to the dining room?" Branden asked. "Your deputies are going to have their hands full."

Robertson stared down at the cars. "Yeah," he said. "But give Sonny, there, some attention first."

13

Saturday, November 2
8:55 A.M.

CAROLINE Branden let herself into Martha Lehman's third-floor dormitory room using a key from Martha's purse. The door opened to the central area of a two-bedroom suite smelling strongly of smoke and stale beer. Caroline negotiated a tangle of cans, pizza boxes, overturned chairs, and a battered coffee table to cross the room and pull up the dusty Venetian blinds on a north-facing window. Behind her, someone coughed, and she turned to see a boy with a patchy brown beard and a sleepy girl wriggle out from under a blanket on a sofa against the wall. With their eyes shaded, they muttered and groaned, and the boy said, "Hey, man," weakly.

The girl stood up and wrapped the blanket around her shoulders, leaving the boy naked on the couch. He sat up grumbling and stood with his back turned to put on a pair of stretched-out jockey shorts.

"Hey, man. What's with the dawn patrol?" he asked and blinked in the strong light at Caroline.

The girl stepped over the mess on the floor and went into one of two bedrooms.

Caroline took off her coat, looked for a place to lay it down, and folded it over her arm. She said to the boy, "I take it this isn't your room."

"Who made you the moral police?" he said.

"I'm Caroline Branden," she said. "I've come to get some of Martha's things."

The boy stood in place for a while as his mind cleared. His eyes focused on Caroline slowly, and he said, "You Doc Branden's wife?" She nodded.

"Oh, crap," he said and pulled tattered jeans off the floor. As he put them on, he said, "Sorry. I didn't know."

He disappeared into the bedroom, and Caroline heard first loud and then hushed voices. When the two emerged, they were dressed.

The fellow said, "I hope this isn't going to be any trouble, Mrs. Branden. I just fell asleep, is all."

The girl, less intimidated, said, "Dr. Branden is Will's professor," and forced a smile.

Will looked sternly at the girl and said, "I was at your home once, Mrs. Branden. I'm Will Bradenton. This is Martha's roommate, Wendy. I don't usually stay if Martha is going to be home at night. Crap. This looks bad, I know. But Martha isn't here."

"Where do you suppose she is, then?" Caroline asked.

"She usually goes out to the mansion with Sonny Favor," Wendy explained.

Will began picking up the mess in the room. Wendy lay casually back on the sofa to light a smoke.

Caroline decided not to mention the murder of Juliet Favor. "I've only come for some of Martha's things."

"That's her room," Wendy said, jabbing her cigarette toward the second bedroom door.

"Thanks," Caroline said.

"Don't mention it," Wendy said, obviously annoyed. "Sit down, Will!" she complained. "Mrs. Branden isn't here to run an inspection."

"No, indeed," Caroline said. She picked her way across the room and turned the knob on the door to Martha's bedroom. Before she opened the door, she turned back to face Will Bradenton. Wendy had moved to the window, where she dropped the blinds with a clatter.

"I've heard mention of your name several times at my house, Mr. Bradenton. Regent's Scholarship, right?"

Will nodded from his position kneeling beside the coffee table. He stood up slowly with several beer cans.

"You're writing your senior thesis, and my husband is, I think, your Second Reader."

"Right," Bradenton said cautiously.

Caroline nodded, paused as if giving that careful thought, and went into Martha's room.

When she turned on the lights, Caroline found a room as ordered and tidy as the front room was a shambles. The aroma of tobacco and stale booze was replaced by a cool and fresh, pungent citrus smell. The bed was made, and the dresser top was polished. The closet doors were closed, and the floor had been vacuumed to trace a star pattern in the carpet. In addition to the bed and dresser, there was a computer on a small brown desk, a tattered recliner, a floor lamp, and a wastebasket. Surrounding these sparse accommodations, there were, on all the walls, covering every available space from floor to ceiling, both black-and-white and color photographs of Amish scenes.

Caroline turned slowly in the middle of the room and studied the pictures. Many of the shots were of buggies traveling away from the lens. A good twenty photos featured horses, mostly Belgian draft horses, and in several of these, small children were at the reins. On the wall over Martha's bed, the photos worked on Caroline's memory to create a curious unease, until she realized they were of places and people she had once known, though not happily. The house and the barns were clearly the ones she remembered from Martha's adolescence, but they had aged rather badly, falling into shameful disrepair, as if time had been a cruel partner with justice. Of the photographs in this group of people, most had been taken surreptitiously, and faces were uncharacteristically prominent, as if Martha had purposefully violated the subjects' privacy. Caroline moved about the room and studied other photos of people, and in all these other cases, the lens had been employed to avoid faces and personalities, more in keeping with Amish prohibitions. But the photographs beside her bed would have been considered profane because the individualities had been so uncompromisingly captured there. Here, Caroline thought, it made sense that Martha would invade and demean, though it was alarming that Martha would have gone back to that part of Holmes County at all.

A cascade of memories spilled over Caroline as she stood alone in the room. There could be no sensible reason for Martha to have gone back. And since she had gone back, the motivation to do so, or the perverse allure, must have been strong. After all it had taken to wrestle her free from that repressive society, and after the dramatic conversion to the Mennonite faith her father and mother had made, it seemed senseless for Martha to have risked the encounter that going back would surely produce. And the struggle there had been a long one, Martha's muteness starting in the first grade. Evelyn Carson had taken years to bring Martha out of the wordlessness, about when Martha's son had been born. Evelyn had always said there were unresolved issues in Martha's life, stemming from her childhood.

With growing unease, Caroline's eyes ran over the faces Martha had captured on film. The older people had changed little in the intervening years. The children she could only guess. But one fellow, though changed, seemed recognizable to her. A man in his twenties, beardless, and apparently happy to have sat for the photo. With a renewed sense of purpose born of disquiet, she turned her attention to the closet.

Into an empty travel bag, she put several dresses, two pairs of jeans, a sweater, and an extra pair of string-tie shoes. At the dresser, she got out black hose, underpants and bras, and two long-sleeved blouses. She put the bag on the bed and stepped back to the closet. Reaching up to the shelves overhead, she took down a heavy camera bag, and carried that to the bed, too. From the photos beside

Martha's bed, Caroline took down the picture of the handsome Amish man in his twenties, smiling clean-shaven from the seat of a hack.

In the bathroom, she found a plastic bucket of toiletries, and this she also carried out to the bed. On going through the contents, she found the box for an Early Pregnancy Test kit. Back in the bathroom, she found a used pregnancy tester in the wastebasket, and her stomach hollowed out like a sinkhole.

14

"I THOUGHT you and Martha were seeing each other," Branden said to Sonny.

When it was apparent that Sonny was not going to respond, Branden said, "Sit up, Sonny. I'm talking to you."

Sonny pulled himself up to sit on the edge of his bed and leaned over with his elbows on his knees. After a minute on the edge of the bed, he straightened his back, looked up at his professor, and said, "Posture."

Branden didn't comment.

"My mother is always correcting my posture," Sonny explained.

Branden nodded slowly. "Your mother called me several times this semester," he said.

"It's the way she said things, mostly," Sonny said. "If just once she could have said she was proud of me."

"Some people just don't show it much, Sonny."

"It makes me nervous being in the same house with her. Always has, even before this. Couldn't really tell you why. Is that normal? I don't think that's normal, Dr. Branden. She wanted me to go to Harvard business school."

"Let's get you through college first, Sonny. Each semester has its own beginning and its own end. So that's all you have to worry about. Do this semester now, and let the other ones come along, in their own time."

"I'm getting a D in chemistry, Dr. Branden. I've got a test on Monday, and I haven't cracked a book."

"I think, under the circumstances, we'll talk to your professor about that. You're in the 11:00 class?"

"Right."

"So that's Professor Pomeroy."

"He's a hard-ass. Won't give anybody a break."

"We can try to postpone your exam."

"Sally had him, too. Got an A in chemistry. She even worked in the lab for him one semester. She's who ought to go to Harvard. Don't know what I want to do. Never have."

"You're not necessarily supposed to know that yet, Sonny."

"A lot of kids know exactly what they want to do."

"That's not you, Sonny. We both know that."

"I'm supposed to run the family businesses."

"Maybe you will. Surely you have plenty of money."

"She's got it set up so that if I don't accomplish certain things, I'll only get an allowance. Mr. DiSalvo had it all in his computer last night."

"Do you want to do those things?"

"I don't believe she ever thought I could."

"That's your mother talking, Sonny, not you."

"She's probably right. God knows how many times she's had to bail me out."

"But you're in college now, Sonny. Make something of that while you can."

"She told me they had to admit me because she's on the board."

"The point is you are here now, and you can decide for yourself what to do with your life."

"She's got it all laid out. If I don't 'measure up,' as she puts it, I'm down to an allowance of . . . She's dead, Dr. Branden."

"Yes."

"It was going to be $4,000 a month, until I was thirty."

"That should be enough for anyone."

"But, eventually, I'll get it all, if I do it her way."

"Do you have any idea how much that will be?"

"It's about $100 million that I know of. The same amount—the other half of a total of $200 million—goes for Sally, but she gets hers outright."

"And what do you have to do for your half?"

"You know. Schools. Run the business. Businesses. And stay single until I'm twenty-seven."

"You never did answer my question about Martha."

"Mom doesn't want me seeing her anymore."

"But that's the thing, now, Sonny. Your decisions have got to be your own, from now on."

"You sound like my sister."

"Martha's very special to me and my wife, Sonny."

"She's told me you gave her one of your scholarships."

"There's more to it than that."

Sonny shrugged.

"You know she's a few years older than you," Branden said

"Yeah, but she's just a sophomore."

"There's still an age difference, Sonny."

"Doesn't seem to bother her."

"Like I said, I expect you to treat her well."

"Last night changes everything. You said that, right?"

"Was she out here with you, Sonny?"

"At first."

"And then what?"

"She had to leave."

"She borrowed your car?"

"Yeah, I told them that earlier."

"Just so we all know that you let her take it."

"Anybody will tell you that."

"Good. Now, why did she have to leave early?"

"Mom didn't get much of a chance to know her."

"Are you making excuses for something your mother did, again?"

"She and Martha had words."

"What about?"

"Me, I think."

"You weren't there?"

"Mom sent me out of the room."

"Then how do you know that's why Martha left early?"

"She told me it'd be no use for her to stay. No use for us to stay together."

"After they talked?"

"Yes. Martha was crying."

"So you let her drive home alone? What kind of a stunt was that?"

"I was expected to stay for dinner."

"You should have done something for her. Sonny, if you've hurt that girl!"

"I didn't know what to do."

Branden drew in a long, calming breath. "Did you see her again, Sonny? Maybe sometime later?"

"No."

"Did she come back out here with your car?"

"No. Like I said, Mother didn't like her much. Mom can be pretty harsh sometimes."

An understatement, Branden thought. He wondered about a boy of eighteen who still hadn't seen his mother for who she was. A kid who a week ago had told his professor he might marry Martha Lehman. Then, the conversation had been about finishing school. Holding off. Caught up in love, Sonny had been very close to chucking it all for Martha.

Was it the $100 million that had turned that all around? Or was it the abiding tragedy, in Sonny Favor's life, of a dead mother's ill-considered and often-stated opinions? "What about Martha?" Branden asked.

"I don't know, Dr. Branden. Maybe we're no good for each other. I've got to think about Mom, now."

Branden held his peace with difficulty.

"When do you think they're going to clean Mom up?" Sonny asked. "They shouldn't leave her looking like that."

15

Saturday, November 2
9:15 A.M.

THE PROFESSOR found Robertson talking with Deputy Stan Armbruster in the pantry adjacent to the kitchen. Armbruster, in uniform, held open a notebook, and was reading from it as Branden walked up. "First officer on the scene was Sergeant Niell," Armbruster told Robertson.

Robertson turned and asked Branden, "What'd you get from Junior, Mike?"

"Nothing, really. He's been here all night, and he let his girlfriend take his car home early last night."

"Don't you think he's a bit too cool, under the circumstances?" Robertson said.

"Sonny has emotional problems in relationships, Bruce. Trouble forming attachments," Branden said. "He's flown back to New York to see his psychologist a couple of times this semester."

"I just think he should be sadder about his mother," Robertson said.

"He wants her cleaned up, mostly. But that's Sonny. He hasn't dealt with the fact that she really is dead."

"Pretty hard to miss," Robertson said.

"Oh, he knows she's dead. He just hasn't let it register at an emotional level. Maybe never will, if his psychologist is right."

"But you said he has a girlfriend."

"He does. At least, I think he does. Sonny can seem normal to just about anyone, and even carry on a love affair, if I'm reading him right. But all the attachments in his life are weak, somehow. If something in a relationship turns sour, he'll pull back from the whole thing. Kind of a 'cut and run' defense against betrayal."

"You his shrink or something, Mike?"

"More like his confessor. But I've talked a lot with his psychologist," Branden said. "His mother had the guy call me the first week of classes. It's all about his childhood. I don't think she knew the psychologist would tell me so much about Sonny's relationship with her, but she's the hub of a very complicated wheel, and Sonny is spinning somewhere out on the rim."

"Go figure," Robertson said.

"I think you may want to talk with his girlfriend," Branden said, tentatively.

Robertson waited a beat, eyeing the professor.

"She's my teaching assistant in Sonny's Freshman Readings seminar."

Robertson raised an eyebrow.

Branden pointed to Armbruster's notebook and asked, "People in the dining room?"

Robertson looked at Branden pensively. "That's all you're going to give us on the girlfriend?"

"I'll bring her down Monday, after classes."

"What's her name?"

Branden hesitated. "Martha Lehman."

"Mike!"

"I know! I know. As far as I can tell, she's just his girlfriend."

"You should have told me this sooner, Mike." To his deputy, Robertson said, "Write that name down, Stan. I'll want to see her ASAP."

"After classes, Monday, Bruce," Branden held firm.

Robertson ran his palm back and forth over his short gray hair. "You're not telling me everything, Mike."

"She's probably more unsettled by Favor's murder than Sonny is right now," Branden said.

"How would she know about Favor's murder this early in the morning?"

"Everyone on campus must know by now," Branden offered.

Robertson's puffy cheeks reddened, and his neck bulged under his collar, signs Branden recognized that the ponderous sheriff didn't like what he was hearing. Signs that, although Robertson might let the topic drop for now, he'd not likely have forgotten that, years ago, Branden hadn't been altogether forthcoming on the troubles that a mute Amish child had overcome. Back then, the sheriff's explosive personality had rankled enough hearts in Martha's Old Order Amish sect to have nearly shut down Branden's investigation for Evelyn Carson into what she thought must be a case of child molestation. Pastor Caleb Troyer, lifelong friend to both Branden and Robertson, had convinced the family of the need to move, and had guided the father to enough of an appreciation of the scriptures that they had converted to the Mennonite faith, at the cost of being shunned by their Amish brothers and sisters. But until he knew more, despite his long friendship with the sheriff, or even because he knew Robertson so well, Branden held back and said only, "After classes Monday, Bruce. That would be best."

Robertson's eyes searched Branden's. Eventually he said, simply, "OK, Monday."

"Right," Branden said.

"I presume you'll still help with our dining room guests?"

"Sure."

"No small children to protect, there?"

"Give it a rest, Bruce."

Smiling, Robertson said, "You're a study, Doc," and winked at Armbruster.

Branden noted the change in demeanor and wondered what traps Robertson had laid in his mind.

"OK. Let's move on," the sheriff ordered. "What do you say, Stan? Who all's in there?"

Armbruster stalled, absorbed in the exchange he had just witnessed.

"The dining room, Stan. You've got a list for us?" Robertson prompted.

"Right," Armbruster said and flipped pages in his notebook. "First, there's the president, Mr. Arne Laughton."

"How long has he been here?"

"He got here early, Sheriff. About 7:30 or 7:35."

"He's been here all morning?" Branden asked.

Robertson rubbed again at the top of his head, and Armbruster said, "Yes."

"Others came out, and then left," Armbruster said. "A William Blake Coffee, for instance."

"Dean of the Faculty," Branden said. "He didn't stay long?"

"In and out at the front door, according to Sergeant Niell," Armbruster said. "The same for a Phillips Royce. In and out about 7:45."

"How about the ones who've stayed put?" Robertson asked.

"Niell sent them around to the back door, and I took them to the dining room."

"Their names, Stan?"

"A Professor Dick Pomeroy, Coach Rebecca Willhite, and then Dr. Royce came back, about fifteen minutes ago."

"When did Pomeroy and Willhite get here?" Robertson asked.

"Right at 8:00."

"Did you take statements?"

"Names, positions at the college, and why they insisted on staying. President Laughton said it was 'to protect the interests of the college.'"

"He's nervous about the financial restructuring Favor had planned," Branden said.

"No need to worry now," Robertson said.

"That's just Arne, Bruce."

Robertson looked at Armbruster.

"Willhite said she was Sally Favor's coach," the deputy said.

"Women's basketball," Branden said.

"And Royce said he was a close friend of the family," Armbruster finished.

Robertson looked at Branden for an explanation.

"He is, or was, Juliet Favor's latest lover," Branden said.

"Sounds to me like you'd enjoy interviewing him," Robertson said.

"Give me Laughton, too," Branden said.

"Then I've got Willhite and Pomeroy," Robertson said. "What's Pomeroy do?"

"Chairman of the chemistry department," Armbruster said.

"The Mad Scientist!" Robertson joked.

"He's pretty sharp," Branden said. "We started together as assistant professors in the '70s."

"Anyone who likes chemistry is already half a flake job, as far as I'm concerned," Robertson said. "Why's he out here?"

Armbruster read from his notes. "He said he had a 9:00 appointment with Ms. Favor and Mr. DiSalvo."

"That makes him an hour early, if he didn't know she was dead," Robertson observed.

"Says he didn't know until he got out here," Armbruster said.

Robertson turned his eyes on Branden.

Branden said, "That's typical Pomeroy, angling to get in early. He probably brought a laptop in case Favor wouldn't see him before 9:00."

"He did," Armbruster said.

Robertson turned for the door to the dining room and said, "You're still on the back door, Stan."

BRANDEN followed the sheriff into the dining room. Laughton, Willhite, and Royce were standing beside a silver coffee urn, near the bay window. Branden saw Royce doctor his coffee from a pocket flask. Professor Pomeroy was seated at the far end of the oval table, punching the keys on a laptop. He glanced briefly at Branden and Robertson, and continued typing.

Branden cut Laughton out of the group, whispering, "Arne, it's horrible," and led the president to the far side of the room. He put Laughton's back to the others and saw Robertson sit at the table with Willhite and Royce. He heard Robertson speak affably, and knew both the coach and the art professor would underestimate the jovial lawman.

"Arne, where does the college stand now?" Branden asked, turning to face Laughton.

"Haven't been able to talk with DiSalvo," Laughton said.

"Do you think they've already executed some of the reorganizations we heard about last night?" Branden asked.

"Don't know, Mike, although from what I heard, if they have gone ahead with it, we're to be cut back about 30 percent overall."

"The history department and the museum were penciled in for 30 percent," Branden said. "Did you get a chance to speak with her after dinner last night?"

"I tried to, Mike, but no."

"Do you know if anyone from dinner stayed late?"

"Maybe Royce. Do you know about them?"

"Everyone does."

"He's an embarrassment. A shameless philanderer."

"But you didn't actually talk to Royce?"

"Couldn't find him, Mike."

"Arne, look. I've got to know if you stayed later than the others. The financial considerations are pretty minor compared to the fact that one of us is likely a murderer. Did you see anyone else who might have stayed later than you?"

"No. There were still two cars left out back, though."

"One of them was yours?"

"I parked in front."

Branden thought and waited.

Laughton realized the problem. "I went to the back, Mike, to try to talk with Bliss."

Branden held silence.

"I hunted him down, Mike, to ask if she'd see me. He was plowing again, in back. There were two cars there, snow covered. When I walked around front, that was plowed out, too, and my car was the only one left."

"So you did stay rather late."

"This place emptied out fast, Mike. I couldn't have waited more than half an hour before I left, and then there were still two cars here. One was Royce's. The other, I don't know."

"How much had Bliss plowed?"

"All of the front, I guess, plus some of the back, by the time I found him."

"What did he say, Arne?"

"Said Favor had a headache."

"You let it go at that?"

"Everyone knows she gets migraines."

"Those bottles?" Branden asked.

"I guess. How'd you know about that?"

"Dick Pomeroy told me about it once," Branden said. "It's DMSO. Helps with chronic headaches, the way he explained it to me. You'd know about it if you had been a hippie, Arne."

"Well, I wasn't."

"They used to put LSD in it and trip."

"I wouldn't know."

"Of course not, Arne. But it's good for headaches. You can still get it at some pharmacies."

"And how did you learn this about Pomeroy?" Laughton asked. He looked over his shoulder at the typing chemist and turned back to Branden.

"Dick likes to talk about his research," Branden said. "And I've been happy to listen. It's really quite fascinating. The college doesn't give him enough credit."

"He gets plenty of money from outside sources," Laughton said. "Favor owns a pharmaceutical company in Japan. He sends them samples for screening."

"Did you know," Branden asked, "that one of his discoveries shows promise as an anti-tumor agent?"

"So that's the Peru angle?"

"He gets his samples there," Branden said.

"I don't think he's spent a summer on campus for fifteen years," Laughton said reproachfully. "Won't serve on faculty committees, either."

"I'd call the latter a sign of high intelligence," Branden laughed. "But, he publishes, Arne. That's good for the college and for the students."

Laughton sighed. "He was just bragging about how many students he's hired on grants over the years."

"How did you get on that topic?" Branden asked.

"He started out saying that Sally Favor, no less, worked with him one summer in Peru, and then in his lab the next semester."

"He took a co-ed to Peru?"

"One summer that I know of, Mike."

Branden encouraged comment by hinting scandal with his eyebrows.

"Oh, no one has to worry about him and Sally Favor, Mike. She's gay—president of the Lambda Society on campus. Becky Willhite is one of the advisers. Sally's also one of her star basketball players."

Branden looked past the president to Robertson, Willhite, and Royce at the far end of the oval dining room table. He said, "I'll bet Willhite took a cutback last night, too."

Coach Willhite, Director of Physical Education, women's basketball coach, and co-adviser for the gay-lesbian Lambda Society, was married, with children, and straight. But her older brother had died of AIDS when she was nine, and she worked with the Lambda Society to honor his memory.

"Why don't you wait around and talk to the sheriff, Arne?" Branden suggested.

"I'll stay until I settle matters with DiSalvo."

"Look, Arne, forget the money for once!" Branden said forcefully.

Laughton shook his head as if to clear his vision and said, "Right. I still can't believe she's dead."

"No, I suppose not," Branden said. "I need to talk with Royce. Can you tell me anything about his reaction to Juliet's murder?"

"He's been drinking already," Laughton said reproachfully.

Branden checked his watch—9:15 A.M.

Over Laughton's shoulder, Branden saw Rebecca Willhite push away from the table where she and Royce had been sitting with Robertson. She looked angry and left quickly. For his part, Robertson looked over at Branden and shrugged. Phillips Royce sat back casually, apparently having enjoyed the exchange between the coach and the sheriff. Robertson got up and loudly said to Royce, "So nice to meet you, Professor," and Branden watched the sheriff amble to the other end of the table to address the chemist Pomeroy, leaving Royce alone for the moment. Branden said goodbye to the president and moved quickly to sit with Royce.

"SHERIFF say something to Coach Willhite?" Branden asked Royce.

"He is rather a blunt fellow, wouldn't you say?"

"More than most. Not as bad as some," Branden said. "I've known him since we were kids, and he has mellowed considerably in recent years."

"Do tell," Royce said, playing with one end of his black mustache. "Look, Mike, this is all rather unnerving, to say the least. Juliet Favor and I were considerably more than friends."

Branden nodded. "You saw her last night?"

"At dinner, like everyone else. But you were there and already know that."

Branden leaned over on his forearms, studied the wood grain in the dining room table, and asked, "I thought you might have come out earlier, or stayed late, Phillips," he suggested.

"I am quite certain that would not be any of your business, Mike, even if you are helping with the investigation of Juliet's murder."

"I guess I'm a little bit involved," Branden said.

Royce tipped his head knowingly. "Did you get anything out of Arne about the cutbacks?"

"We don't know if she signed any papers," Branden said.

"She hadn't," Royce asserted. He took out a pipe with a curved stem and started packing it with tobacco from a leather zippered pouch. Royce lighted the pipe, took several deep puffs, and said, "I doubt the kids will mind a little smoke today."

"You're taking this rather well, Phillips," Branden said.

"I offer no excuses. She was quite aware I didn't love her," Royce said and blew smoke toward the ceiling. "She rather preferred it that way. As for me, I liked proximity to power and money. The sex was agreeable, to be sure," he added wistfully. "I'll miss the finer things that money can buy."

"That's rather cold, Phillips," Branden chided.

Royce leaned forward on the table, planted his elbows, pipe hanging from the corner of his mouth. "Look, Mike," he said. "Juliet Favor took pleasure in only two things. Money and power. And for her, the two were interchangeable commodities. Why do you think she was hounding Arne Laughton about being chairwoman of the board? I was just a diversion. Believe me, there have been others."

Branden took a deliberate pause. Royce sat back and puffed on his pipe.

"Why are you sitting here, Phillips?" Branden eventually asked.

"Morbid curiosity," Royce replied. He stared steadily at Branden's eyes, and then appeared to soften, as if his careful affectations of disinterest had failed him. Eyes lowered, he said, "Truth is, Mike, I can't bring myself to leave." Then, as if that brief moment of honesty were an embarrassment to him, Royce said, "I guess I'm here, like everyone else, for the money."

Branden let that comment hang between them for a moment and said, "I'd be surprised if you're not in her will, Phillips."

Royce stalled, and managed to temper his expression, while

tamping the tobacco deeper into the bowl of his pipe. He took the measure of Branden, took out his flask and drank a swig, and said, unapologetically, "It will augment my salary and endow a few fine arts scholarships. Lord knows they pay us shabbily enough at the college. But, if you've got any suspicions, I'll tell you flatly that my department and my professional work wouldn't have suffered unduly, even if she had lived to implement her new programs. I had no reason to kill her."

"You'll not be surprised to learn, then," Branden said, "that all of the rest of us were slated to take a cutback of 30 percent or so."

"The history department?" Royce asked.

"Also 30 percent. The museum, too."

Royce smiled. "So it wouldn't constitute much of an exaggeration to speculate that you would have had as much a motive for murder as anyone."

"Quite," Branden said. "Quite right. And I guess there's the crux of it. With Favor's dying before implementation of her new budgets, we all are indirect beneficiaries, and indebted to the one person who decided to do more than just talk about it."

"Including the children," Royce added.

"What do you know about them?"

"Very little, actually. Sally I know enough to realize that she disapproves of me. And Sonny—I guess you'll know as well as anyone that he is an insufferable brat."

"Phillips!"

"You serve as his adviser," Royce countered. "Tell me I am wrong."

"You are, to a point," Branden said. "He's—" Branden hesitated, "underdeveloped."

"That boy is mature enough to have wrecked the work of one of my most gifted students!"

"Martha Lehman?"

"The same, Professor. Since they have taken up together, her photographs, when she actually makes any, have been desultory."

"That bad?"

"In the extreme."

"But I thought you considered Martha a natural behind the lens."

"And in the darkroom, Mike. But not anymore. She used to attack a subject like the lens could bare its soul. Profound insight, really. Composition. Point of view. Depth of field, and the technical matters, too. Her best color prints rival Frederic Joy's, for heaven's sake."

"But not lately?"

"Not by the proverbial mile. Last semester she constructed a studio strobe system for studying glass and crystal images. Shapes, color, and lighting. Remarkable, really. This semester, she hasn't logged ten hours on the project. The equipment is dusty, Mike. The studio stays dark."

"And you blame Sonny?"

"No, Professor, I blame you."

"Whatever for?"

"You're the one who introduced Sonny Favor to her."

"I'd hardly put it like that, Phillips. He's just in our class, like anyone else."

"As you say, Mike. But not at all 'like anyone else.' You should have known that a girl with her background would have been overwhelmed by all the trappings of the Favor mystique."

"As far as I know, he only took her to a few Indians games."

"And his Lexus is just a car, Mike. Did you know that his mother bought season tickets for him as soon as he was admitted to our fair college?"

"I don't see that as a problem for anyone."

"Did you know that Sonny took her to New York City?"

"No," Branden answered, on guard.

"She wanted to photograph Ground Zero."

"I knew that, but I didn't know she had actually done it. Not with Sonny."

"He's a profligate moron, Mike, and he's ruined Martha Lehman as an artist. Ten hours in the studio, Mike. That's all I've gotten from her this semester," Royce said. He took off his thick black glasses and polished the lenses with a handkerchief, pipe hanging from his mouth. Folding the handkerchief ceremoniously, the art professor got out of his chair and pointed the stem of his pipe at his colleague. "I don't care if she is one of your projects, Mike. I want her back in the darkroom and the studio, or she's not going to pass my tutorial."

Branden nodded. Changed the subject. "Are you still pressing your motion at faculty meeting?"

"Of course," Royce said. "It is decidedly not fair that the sciences get all that money for lab courses. Other departments have expenses, too."

"I doubt the scientists are trying to get away with anything, Phillips. They've got legitimate expenses."

"Then the science students have got to pay more tuition."

"That's hardly the spirit of the liberal arts."

"Science is not a liberal art."

"It is very much so!" Branden exclaimed.

"Then I will expect you to argue against me tomorrow afternoon."

"Count on it, Phillips."

"If Juliet were still alive, your vote wouldn't count for anything on this issue."

"How so?"

"You would have to ask Henry DiSalvo. But special budgets for the sciences were to be a thing of the past."

"How sad."

"That studio lighting system I told you about?"

"Yes."

"Seem fair to you, Professor, that that equipment came out of my pocket?"

"Not at all, but hurting one branch of the college isn't the way to address the problem."

"When did you cross over to the other side, Mike?"

"Science is the ally of art, Royce. That's the way it's supposed to be."

"Well, it is not my ally. Not in the slightest. It hasn't been, at Millersburg College, for years."

"And you think Juliet Favor had set out to correct that problem?"

"Talk to DiSalvo," Royce said confidently.

"I will."

"Good. And I suggest you stay sharp tomorrow at faculty meeting. I'm not the only professor who feels this way. Not the only one at all."

16

Saturday, November 2
9:35 A.M.

AS THE SKIES cleared briefly, Caroline Branden gunned the engine in her Miata and slid sideways to a stop in the parking lot of Evelyn Carson's building. She got out in deep snow, kicked angrily at the ice packs around her back tires, and then opened the trunk of the car. The bright sun seemed incongruous with the cold air and snow, since to Caroline, after nearly thirty years in northern Ohio, cold weather spoke mostly of cloudy skies.

She popped the zipper of her coat up to the top and pulled her hood over her head. From the trunk of her car, she retrieved the things she had gathered from Martha's room, and closed the lid. Sliding her boots through the snow, she followed the path made earlier to the side door of the Victorian house, and inside, she stomped her feet to knock off snow and ice.

On the second floor, she pushed through the door into Evelyn Carson's office, her arms wrapped around the well-stuffed travel bag, Martha's bucket of toiletries, the camera bag, and a now-wrinkled photograph of a smiling Amish man. She dropped the load on an overstuffed chair and pulled the used pregnancy tester out of her coat pocket. This she placed on top of the pile, noting that Martha's eyes had picked it up immediately.

Evelyn Carson came out of the small office bathroom drying her hands. She saw Caroline, tipped her head toward Martha, and said, "I've got her cleaned up, but she still hasn't said anything."

"Where's her apron?" Caroline asked, keeping her gaze fixed on Martha.

"In the bathroom, here. Haven't dealt with it. I've been trying to talk with Martha, but it's like before. She hears and knows almost everything, but won't respond."

"Not even with her eyes?"

"They track, and the pupils are normal, but they don't register any response to what I say."

"She's afraid to talk?"

"Not quite."

"That's how she was back then."

"That's only partly true. But, today, she seems resolved not to talk. It's not so much a clinical muteness as a willful one. It was like that then, too, only to a lesser extent because she was so young."

"You think she can talk, but chooses not to?" Caroline asked. She took a seat beside Martha and held one of her hands.

Evelyn Carson sat down on the other side of the girl. "She always could talk, Caroline, even then. But like then, I suspect, she has compelling reasons not to talk, now."

"We've got to figure out why, if we're to help her," Caroline said. "Martha, tell us what has happened."

Martha did not turn to Caroline. She stiffened slightly, eyes locked straight ahead. She closed her eyes, drew in a deep breath, and opened her eyes. Slowly, she shook her head side to side, shut her eyes, and this time squeezed them tight.

Caroline looked past Martha to Evelyn and nodded toward the bathroom door. The two got up and opened the door to the bathroom, stepping in. On the back of the door, Dr. Carson showed Caroline where she had hung Martha's stained apron. Then she said, "I checked her car when you were gone."

"Evelyn! We shouldn't be leaving her alone."

"She's not going anywhere. She isn't running from anything, Caroline. It's like before. If she wanted to run away, she wouldn't have come here at all. No. She's protecting someone. There's a reason for her silence, just as there was years ago. She was protecting her younger siblings, then. It was self-sacrificial. It could very well be the same thing, now—protecting herself, or someone else."

"She knows we'll have to turn this apron over to Bruce Robertson, if it figures into his investigation."

"There's blood in her Lexus, too," Carson said.

"It's Sonny Favor's Lexus."

"Well, there is blood in the car. On the steering wheel and on the door handles."

"Lord God. This could mean anything, Evelyn."

"It could mean the most obvious of things. Prepare yourself for the worst," Evelyn said. "Have you spoken with your husband again?"

"His cell is off."

"Great."

"I know. We could call the Favor residence and ask for him."

"If we tell him anything, then he is obliged to report that, right?"

"Yes," Caroline said, following the doctor's train of thought. "OK. Maybe he has done that on purpose, then—switching his phone off."

Evelyn agreed. "The longer he gives us with her, the better it'll be right now. Let's get what we can from her and wait for him to call you."

Caroline pulled strands of her long auburn hair around in front and fiddled with the ends, leaning back against the bathroom sink. Evelyn Carson had been her friend for nearly ten years, Caroline and Mike having helped Martha Lehman when the young teenager had been Evelyn's patient. And the Brandens had seen to Martha's education when she had started college. Now the psychiatrist studied Caroline's eyes and read both present concern and past tragedy, a child in jeopardy being the one thing, she realized, that still could call Caroline's deep faith into question. But where despair might rule, Cal Troyer had taught Caroline to pray, and Evelyn Carson knew that Caroline would again muster unshakable resolve and relentless passion to the cause of Martha Lehman.

Caroline stirred from inward thoughts and said, "I can think of two things to try. Long shots, both, but worth a try."

Back in the office, Caroline took the half-used pregnancy test kit over to Martha and held out the used stick. Then she took out the second tester and handed it to Martha.

Slowly, Martha reached out for the tester and took it in the fingers of both hands. She looked up, first to her psychiatrist and then to Caroline, and sighed. Getting up slowly, she walked to the bathroom, closed the door, and came out some moments later, holding the tester horizontally in front of her. She seemed to stall just outside the bathroom door, and appeared likely to faint. The two women rushed up to her, and each took hold of an arm. With her free hand, Caroline pushed Martha's things out of the chair, and the photograph of the young Amish man caught the air and landed face-up on the carpet several feet from Martha. They eased her down into the plush chair, and Evelyn took possession of the tester. She looked at it, handed it to Caroline, and Caroline confirmed the positive result with a nod. Together, they guided Martha out of the chair and sat her down between them, once again on the sofa.

"How long have you known?" Caroline asked Martha.

Martha said nothing. *Two days,* she thought. *Two days, and the world is upside down. How could She have known? White trash? How could She have said that? All ruined for Sonny. Maybe not, I don't know. What has he done? Will they tell him about me? I almost hope they do.*

"Who knows besides us?" Caroline asked.

Maybe I was always trash. Why else the affair with Royce? No good, backwards, Amish trash. His mother was right. Dead.

"Martha, have you told anyone?" Evelyn pushed.

There was a barely perceptible movement of Martha's head from side to side. *No one knows.*

"Is it Sonny Favor?" Carson asked.

Sonny Favor. Fallen.

Caroline knelt on the carpet and retrieved the photograph she had found hanging in Martha's room. She held it up for Martha and Evelyn Carson to see. "Martha," Caroline said. "It's not him, is it?"

Martha took the photograph tenderly and smoothed the creases, as tears spilled from her eyes.

Dr. Carson said, "You need to tell us, Martha. Have you been seeing John Schlabaugh again?"

But Martha dropped the photograph and buried her face in her hands. A torrent of emotions washed through her, and she seized on the memory of a poem she had written in the sixth grade with Dr. Carson's help.

> *There you are, Dread and Silence;*
> *Twin companions, true.*
> *From this pit I must escape*
> *The shadows—clutching shades of blue.*

17

Saturday, November 2
9:45 A.M.

CAPTAIN Newell waited in the butler's room until the sheriff was finished with Professor Dick Pomeroy and then summoned Robertson through the swinging doors. Robertson pushed through the doors thinking about his conversation with the chemist and saw that Daniel Bliss was no longer with Newell. The muscular captain stood at the sink, wearing latex gloves and holding a green crystal pitcher. "Juliet Favor had her own special pitcher last night," he said.

Robertson glanced at the pitcher and said, "Dick Pomeroy? The chemistry professor? Now there's an interesting fellow."

Newell watched Robertson park his backside on Bliss's desk and said, "Bruce, the pitcher."

Robertson stirred from his thoughts and said, "Sorry, Bobby."

"Juliet Favor reserved this pitcher to herself all last night."

"You got that from Bliss?"

"Only partly. In truth, I got very little from him at all. With his mother dead, 'Mister Favor' is in charge of everything, as far as Bliss is concerned. He made that point very evident."

"What about his sister? She's older than him."

"Bliss wouldn't say."

"Man's startin' to annoy me," Robertson said, and turned with a gunfighter's swagger for the door to the kitchen.

Newell held out his hand and said, "Whoa, Cowboy. You need to hear this."

Robertson stopped, retreated to the desk, and sat back down.

"This is Juliet Favor's *private* pitcher," Newell said with emphasis. "As soon as I asked about it, Bliss dumped the contents into that sink in the wet bar."

Robertson straightened up and waved Newell ahead.

"I've taken it from him for testing. Fingerprints and residue. I've also alerted one of Taggert's assistants to collect the contents of the trap below that sink."

"You say Bliss dumped it out? Was that casual or intentional?"

"He dumped it out just as soon as I took an interest in it."

"Where did you find it?"

"There were two pitchers sitting here from last night. This one, Favor's personal green Tiffany pitcher, and," Newell pointed to a clear crystal pitcher beside the sink, "this other one containing martinis, according to Bliss."

Robertson noted about an inch of colorless liquid in the clear pitcher and asked, "Bliss didn't have a wild hair to dump that one out, too?"

"Just the green one. The one only Juliet Favor used."

Robertson tented his fingers in front of his lips and thought. After a moment, he asked, "What's in the clear one?"

"I'm having it analyzed, too, but that one smells like stale martinis."

"Somebody told me earlier that Favor served martinis before dinner," Robertson said.

"Right. And she gave the appearance of drinking right along with everyone else. But Bliss claims that the only thing in her pitcher was ice water."

"A teetotaler?"

"He claims alcohol worsened her headaches."

"So, she served everybody martinis last night and drank water herself."

"Apparently."

"I wonder how many people knew that?" Robertson said.

"Bliss did, for sure."

"So why did Bliss dump it out?"

"Beats me. But if she took a spill on that marble floor, being drugged from her water pitcher would have made that easier for someone."

Robertson nodded agreement. "Let's wait to see what Missy can tell us about it."

"Do you buy that about the headaches?"

"I reckon so," Robertson said. "I was just talking to Pomeroy, and he confirms what Mike Branden said earlier. Professor Pomeroy came to bring her some headache medicine before dinner last night. He got here early, and Bliss let him set up his laptop in the library for an hour or so before dinner."

"What's your take on the butler?"

"Bliss evidently knows something about the resolution of Favor's estate. Did he tell you anything?"

"Nothing. I asked him a dozen questions if I asked him one, and got nothing from him."

"The Loyal Butler."

"I'll say. If you were to get it from Bliss, you'd think Favor died peacefully, of natural causes."

"Except for that ugly gash at the back of her head," Robertson said sarcastically.

"Have you got anything from Missy Taggert yet?" Newell asked.

"She's still upstairs, so far as I know."

"Well, I'll get this pitcher to her."

"Right. But Bobby, why is Bliss so protective of the children?"

"Maybe he thinks one of them did her in."

"Could be."

"Or maybe he did her, himself."

"He's precise, Bobby. Very precise and extremely careful."

"You think he killed her?"

"If he did, I doubt he'll have made any mistakes."

Newell eyed the green pitcher and said, "Maybe one tiny mistake, Sheriff. By reflex. One impulsive turn of the wrist."

"If he did," Robertson said, "he'll have figured out a plausible explanation for it by now."

18

Saturday, November 2
9:45 A.M.

PROFESSOR Branden got his coat from the chair in the foyer and exited past Niell to the front porch. The cold, dry snow crunched with resonating tones under his boots as he descended the wooden steps. In bright sun on the parking oval in front of the mansion, he slipped his arms into his green and tan parka and zipped it up halfway. With the sun warm on his face, he did not pull up his hood. He fished his cell phone out of a coat pocket and dialed Evelyn Carson's office. Dr. Carson answered.

"It's Mike," he said.

"We knew you would call, eventually. You'll appreciate, I am sure, that it would be a somewhat delicate matter for me to answer certain specific questions about my patient."

"In addition to confidences that a physician would keep," Branden said, "there are, equally, certain questions that I myself would just as soon not have answered at the moment."

"Understood," Carson said. "Here's Caroline."

Branden waited for his wife to answer and then said, "Hold on a moment, I've got company." He pushed mute.

Captain Dan Wilsher approached, ahead of a line of deputies, on the long front drive. The men were spread out, eyes scanning the snow cover as they walked. Wilsher came up to Branden and said, "We're looking for tracks, bloodstains, whatever we might find." He had his hands tucked under his arms to warm them.

Branden asked, "Bruce thinks you'll find bloody rags, that sort of thing?"

"Yes," Wilsher said skeptically. "We've been all through the house and found nothing. Appears there'll be nothing out here, too. Robertson thinks Juliet Favor died when her head hit the marble floor of the foyer, and then someone cleaned up a lot of blood. Trouble is, there isn't any blood. None, at least, that we've been able to find."

"You've tried all the obvious places? Sinks, bathrooms, kitchen, laundry?"

"Right, but we came up with nothing."

Branden cast his gaze around at the smooth snow where they stood and said, "The butler has plowed out here at least once this morning that I know of."

"I know. All the old tracks are gone."

"Blood from last night could still be packed in with the snow-banks," Branden offered.

"Oh, great, Mike," Wilsher said. From his expression, it was clear that Wilsher did not relish having to shovel through the snow.

Wilsher took off his gloves and blew into his cupped hands. "At least, if it stays cold," he said, "the snow won't melt before we get through it all."

Branden said, "Probably wouldn't be worth the time, Dan," and Wilsher grunted displeasure.

"Where's Bruce?" Branden asked.

"He's out back with Bliss and DiSalvo. There's evidently a problem with searching the butler's residence."

Branden nodded and held up his cell phone.

Wilsher said, "Right, I won't keep you," and walked off with his men.

Branden squinted at the morning sun, turned his back to it, and took his phone off mute. To Caroline he said, "Is Martha still there?"

"Yes, we've got her cleaned up a bit, but it wasn't her blood."

"I had assumed she got hurt in a car crash," the professor replied.

"No. There's blood on her apron and on her hands, but she's not hurt. No cuts or scratches."

Branden hesitated, thought. Eventually, he said, "We're looking for blood evidence out here, Caroline. Juliet Favor has a crack in her skull. That's likely how she died."

"You can't think Martha would have done that!"

"Not for a minute. But I've got to tell Bruce about this. Got to tell everyone, Caroline. We're going to have deputies shoveling through snow looking for bloody clothes."

"Wouldn't they have to do that anyway?"

"I suppose. Maybe not. I'm not sure."

"There could be blood somewhere else, too, Michael. I mean, Martha's not necessarily the only one who's got blood on her."

"Sure. We'll look out here. But I've still go to report this."

"What do you want me to do?"

"You've got to keep Martha there."

"The only thing I have to do is keep Martha safe."

"Caroline."

"She didn't do this, Michael."

"OK. I'm not arguing the point. You keep her with you. I'll handle things out here."

"What do you want me to do with her apron?"

"We can't tamper with evidence."

"I know, but I have a clean change of clothes for her, and maybe I could bag the clothes she's wearing."

"Where'd you get the clean clothes?"

"Went back to her room at the college."

"You don't sound too happy about that."

"She's got recent pictures of John Schlabaugh on her wall."

Branden didn't reply.

"Michael?"

"Did she say why?"

"Still isn't talking."

"What does Evelyn say?"

"She thinks Martha chooses not to speak because she's protecting someone."

Branden thought.

"Michael?"

"This is going to be a bit tricky, Caroline."

"You can't think Martha killed her!"

"Of course not. But would you have predicted she'd get in touch with John Schlabaugh? With any Schlabaugh?"

"I don't know."

"Yes, you do, Caroline."

"OK, no. But Bruce will have her locked up if we take her in like this."

"We just won't take her in, then."

"Oh, that'll be a very popular tactic, Professor."

"Just the bloody things go in for now," Branden said. "Get her changed and over to our house. Will Evelyn go with you?"

"One minute," Caroline said. Shortly, she continued. "She says yes."

"OK. Then bag all of her clothes, shoes, stockings, dress, and especially the apron, and put the bag—it should be a clean plastic trash bag—into the trunk of Sonny's car."

"There's blood in the car, too."

"We can't do anything about that."

"What do we do with the car?"

"Put the key under the front seat and leave the car right where it is, unlocked. I'll tell Dan Wilsher where it is, and they can investigate for a while. That should give you more time with Martha. You've got to get her talking before I take her down to Robertson this afternoon."

"You can't do that," Caroline argued.

"I've got to. He already knows she's involved in this some way. I just want us to be the first to know what that involvement is."

"When are you coming home?"

"I don't know. It would be best for me to stay here as long as possible. We're probably going to be at it all day, the way things are going."

"All right."

"Have you got any ideas how to approach Martha?"

"I don't know. She's sleeping on the couch now."

"What did you get so far?"

"She's pregnant, Michael."

"How in the world do you know that?"

Caroline told him.

"This is worse," he said, "much worse."

"She's waking up. I've got to go," Caroline said.

"OK. Get her home, and I'll take care of the car from this end."

Caroline hung up. The professor switched off and pocketed the phone while he walked back along the east drive beside the house. He found Wilsher measuring the depth of a snow pile with a yardstick. The stick and half his arm penetrated the snow before hitting pavement. The captain saw Branden approaching and gave a wry smile. "We're going to have to shovel this out in layers," he said ruefully.

"That's where anything that was dropped on the drive last night is going to be now."

Wilsher acknowledged that by shaking his head, and waved over several deputies. As they came up to him, he said, "We've got to go through all this snow."

One of the men whistled. Another rubbed his forehead with the back of his hand. A third turned away, saying, "I'll look for shovels."

"Try the garage out back," Wilsher said, and motioned for the others to help.

"It's gotten a little more complicated, Dan," Branden said. "Sonny Favor's girlfriend, a student of mine, has shown up with blood on her clothes."

Wilsher gave an incredulous stare.

"We should still look for blood evidence out here, anyway," Branden said.

"Where's the girlfriend, Mike?"

"She's with Caroline and Evelyn Carson. She's evidently in shock."

"She was out here last night?"

"From what I know, yes."

"Does the sheriff know this?"

"That's where I'm headed now. To tell him. Also, we found Sonny Favor's car with its front smashed in."

"Oh, really?" Wilsher said, shading his eyes.

"It's in the parking lot of that pink Victorian house south of Pomerene."

"That's where Carson's office is."

"Right."

"You think the girlfriend drove it there?"

Branden said, "I'm not entirely sure how it got there, Dan, but someone ought to bring it back. Maybe go through it. Caroline bagged Martha's bloody clothes and put them in the trunk. The keys are under the front seat."

BRANDEN rounded the back corner of the Favor house and found several cruisers and cars parked in the snow. Behind a large, four-car garage, he found Bliss arguing loudly with Robertson, in front of the door to the butler's small ranch home.

As Branden walked up, Bliss was saying, "This is my house. You cannot search it without a warrant."

Robertson said, "I'm not going to tell you this again, Bliss. We don't need a dang warrant. This is all part of the Favor estate."

DiSalvo cut in. "The Favors own this house, Bruce, but Daniel has maintained it as a private domicile for eight years that I know of, probably more."

"More than ten," Bliss proclaimed. He pulled the collar of his long dress coat up around his ears and said, "It's cold out here, Sheriff, but I'll not step aside for any reason."

"I'll have you moved!" Robertson barked.

"He's not under arrest, Bruce," DiSalvo said calmly. "And you've no grounds to place him under arrest."

"Obstruction of an investigation will do, for starters," Robertson said, and waved over a deputy.

Branden watched the deputy take out a pair of handcuffs. The professor raised his hand, and said, "Wait a minute, Bruce. You can get a warrant in less than an hour."

Robertson, heated, glowered at his friend.

"Think about it. Without the warrant, your search will be subject to appeal."

Robertson started to speak, but Branden continued. "All we really want to do right now is interview Mr. Bliss. Right? Then, if we get a warrant, all is well and good."

Robertson seemed to relax a degree or two.

DiSalvo said, "You've already kept Mr. Bliss for a good forty minutes. Your Captain Newell did. Do you have more questions, Mike?"

"One or two, Henry," Branden said pacifically.

Daniel Bliss threw up his hands, frustrated.

Henry DiSalvo drew his charges aside on the driveway, and began talking quietly.

Branden pulled Robertson off from the group and told him about Martha Lehman's bloody clothes.

The sheriff asked, "How long have you known?"

"I knew Martha was over at Evelyn Carson's office, and I knew she had wrecked Sonny's car. I just found out that the blood on her clothes isn't her own."

With considerable effort, Robertson forced calm into his voice. "We've been wasting our time out here, Mike!"

"Not at all."

"Oh, really?"

"We need to process this case thoroughly, Bruce. That means doing everything out here that we normally would do. Martha's not talking, so at least for now you won't get anything out of her, anyway."

"Where is she, Mike?"

"With Evelyn Carson. Caroline is there, too."

"Where are the clothes?"

"Dan Wilsher is bringing them in, along with Sonny Favor's car."

"Martha Lehman had the car, like Sonny said earlier?"

"Yes."

"Then what more do we have to do out here? What about Bliss and the Favor kids?"

"It's straightforward, Bruce. I can't believe that Martha Lehman killed Juliet Favor. And even if you suspect she did, you've still got to work the case from every angle. We do the interviews, as we would have done. Missy analyzes the evidence. Then we get to Martha Lehman when Evelyn Carson has her talking again."

19

ROBERTSON led the way into the house by the back door, followed by Bliss, DiSalvo, and Branden. They all labored out of coats, which Bliss hung on the wall pegs near the back door. Bliss, still in his blue jacket and bow tie, leaned back against the center island counter in the big kitchen, and waited with an air of indifference.

The kitchen was rimmed with white counter space and appliances in either brushed stainless steel or glossy black. Two large, double-doored refrigerators stood against the inside wall, next to the rear stairs. Next to them was counter space in the corner and two large stainless sinks along the east wall. More counter space followed to the north wall, where there were two counter-top ranges, with stainless-steel hoods overhead. At the end of the ranges sat Sally Favor, still taking coffee in her bathrobe at a round kitchen table next to the back door.

Robertson waited for DiSalvo to sit at the table with Sally and said, "Miss Favor, if you'll be so kind, I'd like you and Jenny Radcliffe dressed within the hour. And your brother, too. We'll all be going into town before lunch."

Sally glanced at DiSalvo, who nodded consent. She sighed and pushed herself away from the table. The coffee carafe and mug she carried past Bliss to the sinks.

Robertson said, "Nothing in the sinks, please, Miss Favor."

Sally eyed him disapprovingly, set the mug and carafe on the counter, and stomped up the rear stairs without speaking.

Robertson turned a kitchen chair out from the table and sat down heavily. Branden positioned himself in the aisle, where he could observe the expressions of both Bliss and the sheriff.

Robertson pulled at loose skin under his chin and appeared to think carefully before speaking. To Bliss he said, "Captain Newell has taken an interest in Juliet Favor's green pitcher."

"The Tiffany," Bliss commented.

"Precisely. He says you emptied the contents into the sink."

"I did."

"Well, Mr. Bliss, we're pulling apart the trap under that sink, and while I'm at it, I reckon we'll get the traps on the other sinks, too."

Bliss's cheeks heated to pink, but his expression remained stolid. Branden considered the notion that Bliss was worried, but thought, too, that he might simply be embarrassed.

"You want to know why I emptied the pitcher," Bliss said.

"I'd rather know why you didn't empty the other one."

"I would have, if your captain would have permitted."

Robertson waited.

"I was embarrassed that the pitchers had not been cleaned."

"A fastidious butler," Robertson observed.

"I try to be, but yesterday was rather a long day, and Ms. Favor retired early."

"Funny," Robertson said, "that Juliet Favor would serve martinis and keep a pitcher of ice water for herself."

Branden saw a curious movement in Bliss's eyes.

"She has been alcohol intolerant for many years," Bliss said.

Robertson turned to DiSalvo, who said, "It's true, Bruce. She kept it very private. I am sure not even the children knew."

"You seem to know a lot about the lady," Robertson said.

"When my wife was still alive, we were close friends of both Harry and Juliet Favor."

"So, she drank water?" Robertson pressed.

"Chilled well water," Bliss said.

"And nobody knew?" Robertson asked.

"Most anyone will have observed that she drank from a separate pitcher, but such indulgences are not uncommon among the very rich," Bliss said.

Robertson nodded as if conceding the point. "I'm curious to know what cleaning you did before my sergeant first arrived," he said, eyes fixed on the floor at his feet.

Branden watched Bliss closely, and saw no untoward reaction.

"Why, none, of course," Bliss replied. "I expected to find Ms. Favor in the library. Perhaps the kitchen. She's an early riser. But, once I did find her, I touched nothing."

"Quite the expert trooper, aren't you, Mr. Bliss," Robertson challenged.

"I've watched my share of *NYPD Blue*."

"I like Sipowicz, myself," Robertson said.

"I'm not surprised," Bliss said.

"So where did all the blood go, Detective Bliss?"

"I am quite certain I do not know," Bliss said. He pushed himself away from the island counter and stepped to the sinks, where he retrieved a wrinkled hand towel from the countertop, and came back to his original position.

"Where were you when Sonny called 911?" Robertson asked.

"In my home." The towel got folded neatly and was laid carefully on the counter.

"How convenient," Robertson said.

"I see no reason for sarcasm," Bliss said coolly.

"Were the doors locked or unlocked when you came into the house?" Robertson continued.

DiSalvo said, "I think this has gone on quite long enough."

"No, it's OK," Bliss said. "Unlocked, Sheriff."

Robertson waited for an explanation. None was forthcoming.

"Isn't that a bit unusual?" Robertson finally asked.

"Not for the Favors."

"All of them?"

"The children have frequent parties when Ms. Favor and I are away."

"And they don't lock the doors?"

Bliss shrugged.

"What about Juliet Favor? She in the habit of sleeping with the doors wide open?"

"Not in the least."

"So, you'll admit it is unusual to find the doors open. Was that the front door, too?"

"Front and back."

"I presume the alarms were off, too," Robertson added.

"Evidently," Bliss said.

Robertson pulled at an ear lobe.

Said Bliss, "I would characterize that as unusual, but not noteworthy."

"Imagine how pleased I am to have your assistance," Robertson shot.

Branden suppressed a smile with difficulty. DiSalvo said, "Stop it, Bruce."

"My apologies, Mr. Bliss," Robertson said with a wave of his hand.

Bliss remained implacably silent.

"Who comes out to these parties?" Robertson continued.

"I wouldn't know. College students."

"Which is it? 'You wouldn't know'? or 'college students'?"

"I only presumed."

"How many times did you plow last night?"

"Two or three."

"Which is it? Two or three?"

"Three, last night. Twice before dinner, and once after. Once again, this morning, before sunrise. That was before I entered the house."

"Did you see anything unusual this morning?"

"Mr. Favor had parked his car at the front."

"Why is that unusual?" Robertson asked, turning his eyes to Branden.

"Because I don't believe it is there now," Bliss said.

Robertson's neck thickened like a charging bull, and Branden knew why. A brief silence passed, the sheriff staring at the professor. Bliss noticed the look and stood up straighter, attentive.

Branden said, "Dan Wilsher has the car now, Bruce."

Robertson's expression did not soften. "Where is Sally's car?" he eventually asked Bliss.

"She keeps a BMW in the garage."

"Is it there now?"

"I believe so. Also Mr. Favor's 4x4."

"Last night, Mr. Bliss. Who was the last to leave?"

"I spoke with President Laughton, and I presume he left. Then there was one car left in the back, Royce's."

"And out front?"

"I didn't look."

"Did you go through the house before you turned in?"

"No."

Abruptly finished, Robertson said to Branden, "Do you have anything further, Professor?"

Branden thought and asked, "Who were the first to arrive?"

"Mr. Favor and his girlfriend. Professor Pomeroy—I had asked him to come out early. Mr. DiSalvo. President Laughton. Dr. Royce. Then everyone else arrived at about the same time."

"Sally and Jenny?" Robertson asked.

"I think they were here most of the day," said Bliss. "I did not see them arrive."

20

AT THE BRANDENS' home on a cul-de-sac near the college, Caroline seated Martha at the kitchen table and put on a pot of coffee. From the many dozens of mugs she had collected over the years, she selected three—a scenic Badlands, a Niagara Falls, and a Lincoln. She carried the mugs to the kitchen table and found Martha standing at the window, gazing at a woodpecker on the feeder just beyond the storm windows of the long back porch. To Caroline, Martha's posture seemed more relaxed. Caroline stood quietly beside the table and signaled Dr. Carson with a finger to her lips.

Martha watched the birdfeeder for several minutes after the woodpecker had left, and then stirred. She turned to face Caroline and Evelyn and looked at each of them. Stepping away from the window, she came around the large table and walked into the Brandens' family room. There she stood in front of the fireplace, eyes fixed on a Civil War musket on the mantel. Familiar with the room, Martha dropped casually into a recliner. She used the remote to switch on Fox 8 News from Cleveland, and idly watched a forecast calling for continued cold, Saturday morning, skies graying, as another storm approached from the northwest for Saturday night.

Back in the kitchen, Martha accepted a mug of coffee from Caroline and sat opposite the two women at the rectangular table. Her eyes settled on the elaborate grain in the curly maple tabletop, and she listened to Caroline and Evelyn as she took an occasional sip of coffee.

Said Caroline, "Martha, let us help you."

Evelyn tried, "Martha, tell us about the blood."

Martha gazed a long time into Dr. Carson's eyes, and then turned away, silent.

After a dozen or so further questions, Caroline shook her head and signaled Evelyn to follow her to the living room. She drew back drapes to let in strong morning sun, and sat on a couch next to Martha's purse, which they had found in the Lexus. "I feel like such a snoop," she said to Evelyn, who swept her fingers forward to encourage Caroline.

Caroline emptied the contents of the purse onto the coffee table, and she and the psychiatrist knelt on the carpet to go through the items. Aside from the usual things, they found a fat leather folder holding pictures, a little blue notebook with phone numbers and handwritten notes in different inks, a cell phone and its charger, and a laminated table of photographic data, which Martha had evidently made for herself on a computer. Caroline started paging through the blue book, and Evelyn turned the cell phone on.

Most of the numbers Caroline found were listed beside names —friends, professors, relatives. Two numbers were listed without names. To Evelyn, she said, "See if this one is in that phone's address book." She held the little blue spiral notebook so Evelyn could see the number.

Evelyn punched keys and said, "The Martins. It's a Canton exchange."

"It was Martins who adopted her child," Caroline said. "Steve and Becky Martin."

"Do you think she will have been in touch with them?" Evelyn asked.

"Could have been."

"That would carry a significant emotional price," Evelyn said.

"Try this number," Caroline said, and showed Evelyn the book again.

Evelyn scrolled through the address book, and after a minute or so, said, "It's listed simply as 'John.'"

Caroline stood up and took the phone. In the kitchen, she showed the display to Martha and gently asked, "Is that who I think it is?"

Martha looked dispassionately at the listing and said nothing.

Caroline scrutinized Martha's expressionless features and then pushed SEND, holding the phone to her ear. Evelyn Carson sat down to listen to Caroline's half of the conversation. Martha looked away.

"Hello," Caroline said. "I presume you are John Schlabaugh?"

"Caroline Branden."

"Yes, I am sure you do, Mr. Schlabaugh, and let me assure you I remember you very well, too."

"No, but I wouldn't call you on her behalf, for anything."

"Why?"

"That would be out of the question."

"You tell me."

"I only want to know why she's been calling you."

"I don't believe that."

"No. It's preposterous."

"I'll do no such thing."

"No. You listen. Martha may be in some kind of trouble. She's not talking again."

A pause.

"I don't believe you."

"Not Martha. Me."

"When?"

"Where?"

"Count on it, Mr. Schlabaugh."

She switched off and very slowly put the phone on the table.

"It sounds as if you're going to meet him," Evelyn said.

"Tomorrow is an off Sunday for Amish."

"He's willing to talk?"

"Says he's eager to!" Caroline exclaimed. "That takes some nerve."

Evelyn nodded.

"I said I'd go down to Charm, tomorrow," Caroline explained "To meet him in the parking lot of that old cheese factory at 2:00 P.M."

"I'll go with you."

"He said just me."

"I don't care."

"OK, but I've got a thing or two to say to him."

"OK. But first, you're going to have to hear some things that perhaps you'll find surprising. You don't know the whole story about John Schlabaugh."

Martha watched the two women silently. *It wasn't John. Don't blame him. He took me away. He made it stop. Chased the blue shirt away.*

21

SALLY and Jenny descended the front staircase of the Favor home dressed in blue jeans and colorful sweaters. They each had a winter coat, and they held matching wool caps. They also each held a cigarette, Jenny a lighter, too. They came up to Ricky Niell at the front door waving their cigarettes, and Sally said, "Good morning, Officer."

Niell said, "It's Sergeant. Sergeant Ricky Niell."

Jenny said, "Officer Ricky. Now that's a nice name, isn't it, Sally?"

Sally said, "Sergeant, please tell the Oaf Sheriff that we'll be on the front porch."

Niell opened the door for them and stepped outside to hold it open while they exited. "Oaf is right," he said. "You got another one of those?"

Sally and Jenny exchanged amused glances. Jenny took out a pack and offered a cigarette to Niell. He took it, and she lighted it for him. Niell drew on the cigarette as if he had needed a fix all morning. He closed the door and stayed outside with the women.

On the shaded front porch, the snow had not melted. On the parking oval below the porch, patches of blacktop showed, where Daniel had plowed, and there the snow was melting slowly in the sun. Niell stepped to the far end of the porch, and, to the west, he saw dark clouds approaching. Blowing smoke into a crisp westerly breeze, he said, "Sheriff Robertson is a piece of work."

"I'll say," Sally said and approached Niell, kicking snow with her boots. "He's a colossal bore."

Niell turned to face her on the porch. "I don't think he has a handle on the finer points of this case," Niell commented. "And please let me say, I am sorry about your mother."

"I'm not," Sally said hotly. "She was a hypocrite."

Niell waited.

Sally said, "Do you know how many affairs she's had on campus?"

Niell shook his head and watched Sally's eyes intently.

"Three in ten years, that I know of."

"Wow," Niell said. "You know that for sure?"

"Pomeroy and Royce were just the latest," Sally said pointedly. "If she's said it once, she's said it a thousand times. 'All I want is for a man to be strong.' Please! What a whiner. She's the biggest castrater I know."

"Or she was," Niell said, hoping to get a reaction.

"Was. Yes, was. She's got my brother cut back to a spineless brat, and Royce, her latest, is a stumble-down drunk."

Niell's mind raced to anticipate what to say next, to keep her talking. "I don't think she would have liked our sheriff," he said, laughing.

Sally smiled. "She'd have taken him on, all right. The most competitive bitch I know." She drew long on her cigarette and exhaled slowly. "You think it's right, Sergeant Niell, that a mother would find it necessary to compete with her children?"

Niell shook his head.

"She's all hammers and nails," Sally said. "Tough, or so she thinks. 'I'm a survivor.' God, how sick I am of hearing that."

Niell crushed out his smoke on the porch railing and said, "It sounds like she had it tough."

"Maybe as a child, but not after she married. Not then at all."

"My old lady was like that, too," Ricky lied.

Sally said, "She was cruel. You should have heard her bawling out Martha Lehman. 'White Trash' this, and 'Country Trash' that."

"Is that Sonny's girl?"

"If he has the brains to keep her," Sally said.

"Is she a pretty nice girl?"

"Yeah, sure. I guess. Kinda simple. But, my mother thought she had her number. Told her she was no good for Sonny. Told her she knew about her 'dalliance' with Professor Royce. Bawled her out something fierce, and told her that if she didn't break it off with Sonny, she'd have her ruined at school."

"Whew, what a —," Niell said. "Where'd she get off talking like that?"

"If you look like you stand half a chance of costing my mother money, she'll claw your eyes out."

"How did you hear them?" Niell asked. He knew instantly that he had wrecked the flow of the conversation, so he quickly said, "Say, can you spare another smoke?"

Jenny handed over her pack, and Niell knocked one out. He bent low and cupped his hands around Jenny's lighter, and puffed. When he looked up, Sally was gazing at the dark clouds in the west, and her eyes had moistened.

"I've been on a yo-yo string all my life," she said with her back turned. "Trying to win her approval, and then giving up. And trying again because I couldn't help it." She turned around, crying. "That's Sonny's problem. He hasn't given up. Nothing could ever be good enough for Mother. So I quit trying. Sonny's never going to make it on his own."

Niell knocked ash off his cigarette and held Sally's eyes sympathetically. Sally grew quiet and drew inward. Jenny went to her and embraced her as she continued to cry softly. Niell leaned against the railing and waited.

After a while, Jenny held Sally at arm's length and said, "It's over, Sally. She's gone."

Sally lifted her head and dried her tears on the sleeve of her coat. Niell produced a handkerchief and said, "Keep it."

Sally used it and stuffed it into the pocket of her coat. "I don't know why I told you that, Sergeant. I hope it won't be used against me in a court of law."

Niell laughed. "Nothing of the kind," he said.

"Thank you," Sally smiled.

The two women descended the porch steps and walked around the front corner of the house, toward the back. Niell found a bottle of mouthwash in the back bathroom on the second floor and took it out on the front porch. There, he rinsed until he could no longer taste tobacco.

22

SHERIFF Robertson met Sally and Jenny as they rounded the back corner of the big house. Waiting next to the cars and cruisers were Daniel Bliss, Henry DiSalvo, Mike Branden, and Sonny Favor. Several deputies worked with shovels in the snowbanks beyond.

"Ready to go, girls?" Robertson asked. "It's still an hour or two before lunch. Maybe we can finish up at a decent hour."

DiSalvo stepped forward and said, "First, I'll have a word with Sally and Sonny." He waved them over to the far edge of the parking lot and began to speak softly to them next to the family limousine.

Jenny Radcliffe found herself alone with the sheriff. She leaned back against his black-and-white cruiser and lit another cigarette.

Robertson pointed at the Favors, talking secretively with DiSalvo, and said, "They're cutting you out of the play. Bluebloods stick together."

Radcliffe laughed outright and wagged her finger at the sheriff. "Nice try, Mr. Policeman," she said.

"Sally is in more trouble than you realize, young lady."

"Don't you 'young lady' me, old man," Jenny barked, heated. "I don't tolerate fossils like you."

"Well, I'm sorry," Robertson said, feigning astonishment. "I only meant that you are over here, and they are over there."

"Sally will call me when she wants me."

"Is that how it works, then? You're her little pet?"

Radcliffe threw her cigarette down and crushed it hard under her boot. "I know what you're trying to do."

"I'm trying to tell you what kind of trouble you three kids are in."

"I already know that."

"We know about Sally's fight with her mother."

"That's not news."

"We also know that Sally was going to be cut off. A busted trust. No inheritance."

"That's not the way it is. Sally will be fine. She talked to Mr. DiSalvo in the kitchen."

Robertson unzipped his coat and reached into the breast pocket. He pulled out a small notebook and read some figures there. He angled the page so Jenny could see the numbers, and said, "Cut from a trust fund worth $10,250,000 now, to $4,000 a month until she's thirty. That's a motive for murder."

"Sally hasn't been cut out of the will. She gets almost half of everything."

"And how do you know that?"

"Like I said, she talked to Henry DiSalvo."

"What did you two overhear last night to cause Sally to take on her mother that way?"

"You already know."

"Busting Sally's trust?"

"Yes."

"There has to be more."

"Well, there isn't."

"You're lying. You were drunk."

"I was with Sally. We stayed by ourselves all night. Partied in her room."

"You must have slept some."

"Not really."

"Yes, really. Then, sometime later in the night, closer on toward morning, Juliet Favor went downstairs, and Sally knocked her down on the marble floor. Then you two carried her upstairs, and left a blood trail in the staircase carpet."

"I don't have to take this," Jenny said.

Robertson decided that he had her about as worked up as he wanted and said, "Then Sonny is the only one who could have killed her."

Jenny looked over to Sally and Sonny, who were still talking to DiSalvo beside the black limousine. She glowered up at Robertson and said, "Neither one of them killed her."

"They benefit from her death, equally. That means they had equal motive to have wanted her dead. You say you were with Sally all night."

"It's the truth."

Robertson put his notebook away and zipped up his coat. "We will continue this in town."

Jenny Radcliffe squared up to the big man, gave him the finger long and steady, and started off in the direction of the limousine.

Robertson caught her coat sleeve and said, "You're not riding with them."

She jerked loose and stood her ground, saying, "Oh, yes I am."

Ricky Niell came around the corner of the house and sized up the standoff. He said, "She can ride with me," and Robertson saw Radcliffe relax a bit.

"OK," Robertson said dismissively. "You ride with Sergeant Niell."

Radcliffe moved two steps in Niell's direction, and Niell said, "This way, Jenny," pointing to the cruiser nearest the back door.

DiSalvo noticed the skirmish and had made it to Robertson as Niell was leading Radcliffe to his car. To Robertson, DiSalvo said, "Jenny Radcliffe is represented by Baker, Lumbaird, and Drumond, out of Wooster. The Favor children have just retained them on her behalf." To Jenny, DiSalvo added, "You should not say anything until your lawyers are present, Jenny."

Robertson said, sarcastically, "Now see, Jenny. They've gone and made this all adversarial."

Radcliffe pulled an imaginary zipper across her lips and smiled at DiSalvo before getting in the front of Niell's black-and-white.

DiSalvo told Robertson, "She's not to be questioned," and walked back to the limousine. Robertson watched the three climb in the back. Bliss closed up and got in behind the wheel. When Niell pulled out, Bliss followed.

Alone on the packed snow stood Robertson and Branden. The sun was up at its midmorning position, but clouds were swarming in from the west on a cutting wind. Robertson put on gloves and smiled.

Branden shook his head. "You were working her pretty hard, Bruce."

"I'm just warming up."

"We're going to have to keep them separated down at the jail."

"I've already called Ellie. She's setting up Interview A and B, and we can use my office, too. You gonna help?"

"I'd like to, but what's with you? You don't seem like yourself."

"It's nothing, Mike. Now, what have we got so far?"

"We know who was here, and when," Branden said.

"For the most part. But, there's still that little matter of the Lexus that seems to move itself from place to place."

Branden ignored the thrust. "We also know when everyone left."

"Except that Bliss didn't sweep through the house before he turned in."

"We do know that Sally, Jenny, and Sonny stayed the night," Branden said.

"And we know someone cracked Juliet Favor's skull."

Branden shook his head. "Trouble is, there are a good fifteen people with motive to have done that."

"I put it at more like twenty."

"So, motive won't solve this one," Branden said.

"Not at first. Someone has to make a mistake," Robertson said.

"Do you know when Missy and her people will be done in the house?"

Robertson checked his watch. "In about an hour. By noon, anyway."

"Her station wagon is out front. Who else is still here?"

"My photographer just left," Robertson said. "There are still two tecs with Missy."

"She knows about the pitcher?"

"Right. There's something else."

Branden waited.

Robertson took off his hat and rubbed the top of his head with a gloved hand. "I'm having them test a little bottle labeled DMSO."

"Pomeroy's medicine?"

"She was dabbing that stuff on her temples all night long."

Branden said, "Then I'll see you in town," and started walking toward his car beside the garage.

Robertson looked suspiciously at the professor's vehicle and said, "That a new one?"

"No."

"How many cars do you have, Mike?"

"This is just our little around-town sedan."

"How many? Give!"

"I still have the truck."

"OK."

"We also have our custom van."

"Tough life."

"There's Caroline's Miata, too."

"Four. You've got four cars."

"Yeah, I guess so."

"Geez, Doc. Have you been taking money from Old Lady Favor, too?"

23

Saturday, November 2
11:00 A.M.

CAROLINE and Evelyn moved Martha to an upstairs bedroom, and she was asleep by the time they had pulled the covers up over her shoulders. Evelyn went downstairs to make another pot of coffee, and Caroline lingered in the bedroom doorway, watching Martha sleep.

It had been nine years since Martha's son had been born, and Caroline now bitterly remembered the day John Schlabaugh had brought her in a flatbed wagon to the emergency room of Joel Pomerene Hospital. Caroline had been a volunteer in pediatrics, and Martha had been fourteen.

The mad scramble in the emergency room was lodged vividly in Caroline's mind. The filthy clothes they had cut away. The Cesarean section to save the child. The transfusions as Martha had bled out on the table. All these played again in her memory, like an old movie, scratched film on a tattered screen, as Caroline fingered the veins in her arm where they had taken blood for Martha. When she realized she was crying, Caroline went to the bathroom, dried her eyes and blew her nose, and went down the steps angry again at the backward Amish peasant doctrines that had nearly cost child and mother their lives.

In the kitchen, Caroline rinsed out her Lincoln mug and poured herself a cup before the coffee had finished brewing. Evelyn, watching, read the expression on Caroline's face and anticipated the need to talk about matters that had been left unsaid over the years.

"You may have been too hard on John Schlabaugh, Caroline."

Caroline bristled instantly. "He nearly killed her!"

Evelyn refrained from comment, and Caroline sat down at the table, heat dissipating quickly from her cheeks. "I'm sorry, Evelyn. I was there when he brought her in, lying in the back of that wooden cart like something out of fifteenth-century Europe. My land, Evelyn, she was nearly dead."

"Another way to look at it is that he actually saved her life."

"How can you say that? He had her God knows where for three months, and you yourself swore out a complaint as her psychiatrist."

"Her parents always maintained that they knew where she was, and that John Schlabaugh was engaged to her and was caring for her as they wished."

"He used a midwife, Evelyn. They almost killed her."

"I haven't told you everything, because after she got to know you, she asked me not to."

"Do you know that the only support that she got from her so-called Amish Brothers and Sisters," Caroline said, "was the bishop showing up once at the emergency room? We didn't know if she would live or die, and there stood that sanctimonious creep with two pillowcases full of money. 'We pay cash' is all he said. Turned and walked away like he had done nothing more than talk to a bank teller."

"What you don't know is that John Schlabaugh helped pay her psychiatric fees when her family was shunned for buying a car."

"You mean turning Mennonite," Caroline said.

"It's all the same to Amish. Once you're out, they're off of you like a dirty shirt."

"It's too harsh, Evelyn. How many poor souls get cut loose like that every year? They never seem to make it, out in the world."

"When they find a new church home," Evelyn said, "they seem to be OK."

"Then thank God for Cal Troyer."

Evelyn let a silence pass and then gently said, "Did you know that, when Martha first started talking again, it was to John Schlabaugh?"

Caroline started crying, and Evelyn reached across the table to take her hand. "Caroline," she said. "I'm going to tell you everything I can about Martha Lehman without breaking her confidence. You know most of this, but you need to remember before we talk to John tomorrow.

"I first saw Martha when she was nine years old. It was spring. Her father brought her in and said, 'You are a head doctor. Make her talk.'

"For five years, I saw her every week, and she never said a word. So I devised other ways to draw her out. I brought her brothers and sisters into her sessions, and without exception, she was cold toward her older siblings and protective of the younger ones.

"I'd start poems for her, and she would write out the finish to them. We worked jigsaw puzzles, and as soon as she got the border finished, she would lose interest.

"By the time she was fourteen, I had concluded that she had been sexually abused as a very young child, perhaps as early as five years old, and that she was in jeopardy again as a teenager. That's when I told the parents they should move. That's when Cal Troyer got involved. He helped them understand how they could make a change and not forsake their faith. The bishop had them convinced that to leave an Amish sect meant a total loss of faith. At that point, she had her child."

"It's John Schlabaugh's," Caroline said.

"I'm not so sure anymore."

"It'd be easy enough to tell," Caroline said.

"Schlabaugh is Amish. He'd never agree to a blood test."

Caroline drew her hand away from Evelyn's and dried her eyes with a napkin from a wooden holder on the table.

Evelyn continued. "After her son was born, I saw Martha for another year and a half. Like I said, she first started talking to John Schlabaugh. He'd bring me bits and pieces of what she said. I won't go into everything, but by the time she finished with me, she was talking freely, and went home to her newly-turned-Mennonite family. You picked up with her after that."

"She got her G.E.D.," Caroline said. "She's on one of our scholarships."

"I know."

"I hear a 'but' in there somewhere."

Evelyn locked her fingers together on top of the table. "There was always more work to do, Caroline, even before this episode."

"You said she talked freely."

"We never addressed her real problem."

"What does that mean?"

"She's still vulnerable to the deep psychological consequences of some early childhood episode. Her silence now may have been triggered by something else, but she still faces the need to confront old issues. Her memory will eventually bring it back. This new pregnancy may be the thing that has put her into relapse. Or the Favor murder could have done it. But, until her mind and heart are strong enough to handle the pain, she won't be able to remember her childhood. And until those memories are cleansed, she can't be truly healed."

"How long could that take?"

"Some people don't recover memories of severe abuse until they are forty or fifty. Then their world caves in, and they don't know why. In therapy, sometimes, survivors can work through the trauma that they, as children, could never face."

"And you think Martha is like that?"

"Very possibly. All we really know is that she's not talking again."

"You said she's protecting someone."

"That someone may be the very small and helpless Amish girl of five she used to be."

24

PROFESSOR Branden stopped at home on the college heights at the east edge of town and spoke briefly with his wife and Evelyn Carson, confirming that Martha was sleeping and, for the present, safe.

At the courthouse, he found the long Favor limousine parked along the east sidewalk, blocking the spots at the hitching rail reserved for buggies. A county worker in tan Carhartt coveralls was tucking a note under the wiper blades on the driver's-side windshield.

Branden drove around behind the red brick jail, parked beside the bank building in an alley that had been plowed, and went up the short stack of concrete steps into the back of the jail, passing a man shoveling off the last patches of ice. The back door put Branden inside a long hallway. To his immediate left was the squad room, with lockers for the deputies and desks for the family court detectives. On his right were the doors to Interview A and B. He poked his head into B and found the Favor children, with lawyer DiSalvo, seated around a rectangular gray metal table, their winter coats hung over the backs of their chairs. They had been talking when Branden had opened the door, but fell silent as soon as they saw him. DiSalvo said, "Mike, can you hurry this along?"

Said Branden, "I just got here, Henry. I'll track down Robertson, and then we'll get you all home as soon as we can."

In Interview A, Branden found Ricky Niell talking with Jenny Radcliffe. Her winter coat was piled on top of the metal table, and she was fiddling with her cigarette lighter. She glanced up forlornly at Branden, and Niell gave a little wave, indicating that they were fine for the moment just talking.

Further down the hall, Branden passed Robertson's office, door closed, on the left, and at the end of the hall he found Ellie Troyer-Niell in a long, flowered dress, putting her hair up in a bun. She smiled at him with her hands behind her head, working pins into her hair. Finished, she came out from behind her counter and hugged the professor. Leading him by the arm, she sat him down in her office chair beside a desk banked with radio electronics and stuck her left hand under his nose. "What do you think of those?" she asked, and waved her fingers in front of his eyes.

Branden wobbled his head as if dizzy and took Ellie's hand to inspect the diamond ring and wedding band. "Very nice," he said, and kissed the back of her hand.

On the intercom speaker, they heard Robertson say, "Ellie?" from his office. She pulled Branden out of her chair, sat down, pushed a button, and said, "Doc's here, Sheriff. You think we ought to keep him, or chase him back up the hill?"

They heard Robertson bellow through the thin, pine-paneled wall. "Tell him he's under arrest for conspicuous consumption in a recession. Man's got four cars, Ellie."

Branden leaned toward the microphone and motioned for Ellie to hold the button down. "And you and Missy have made how many trips to Chicago this year? I hear it's the Chicago Renaissance Hotel, no less."

"I like that town," came the answer. "And how's about some coffee in here?"

Ellie switched off, and walked Branden back down the hall to Robertson's door, carrying a carafe of fresh coffee from the maker on her desk. She pushed through the door ahead of the professor, took a mug from Robertson's credenza, and poured coffee for

Branden. Then she went around the room, giving refills to Captains Newell and Wilsher. She stopped last at Robertson's massive cherry desk and sat on the corner there, waiting for all the world as if she expected Robertson to say something pleasant. Robertson held out his coffee cup and said, "Please," and Ellie poured out the last of the brew. At the door, she turned, said, "I've seen all of your suspects, Sheriff. They don't look like killers to me," and left.

Branden took off his coat, held it across his lap, and dropped into a leather chair in front of Robertson's desk. Wilsher was seated to Branden's left. Newell stood by the north windows of the large corner office, gazing out at the snow. Before anyone could speak, Ricky Niell came in, closed the door, and said, "I don't think Jenny Radcliffe is going to tell us very much."

Robertson leaned back heavily in his swivel chair and balanced his coffee cup on his belly. "Odds are she didn't kill Favor," he observed. "For now, let's get our facts straight, before we talk to any of them further." To Branden he said, "Then I'm gonna want to see your Martha Lehman." To everyone, he added, "In the meantime, we run everything else, just like we would normally do."

"Assuming Martha didn't kill Juliet Favor," Branden corrected.

"For now, at least," Robertson agreed.

Ricky pulled a chair away from the wall where Robertson had tacked up his collection of law enforcement arm patches, sat down, straightened the creases of his uniform pants, and said, "That whole house was wide open when I got there, and I think it probably was unlocked all night, too."

"That agrees with what Bliss told me," Newell said. He sipped some coffee, turned away from the windows, and took a seat to Branden's right, facing the sheriff. "Four or five people could come and go, front and back doors and all, plus two separate staircases, and they might never see each other."

"The house is noisy," Branden said. "You can easily hear what's going on in the next room."

Newell said, "The intercom system can be set so you could hear a conversation on the first floor while listening from the second or third floor."

"What's on the third floor?" Robertson asked.

"A workout room and a sauna," Newell said. "It's pretty nice. And she's got a workout schedule tacked to the wall that would tire out a horse. She's got a chart on the wall, where she has been marking off reps for each workout. She had to be in great shape."

"You'd know if anyone would, Bobby," Robertson said.

Branden asked, "Do I have it right that Sally Favor overheard her mother talking to Sonny about the kids' trusts?"

Niell said, "Right. She was going to put them on an allowance, rather than let them have their money."

Robertson said, "Jenny doesn't think Sally will lose a dime, once the will is executed."

Observed Niell, "They didn't know that last night."

"Right," Robertson said. "So that might have been a motive at the time. That and two dozen others. But mother and daughter had a fight over it in front of Henry DiSalvo. I'm sure he could tell us a thing or two about that family."

"It's more complicated than just the family," Branden said. "Even professors are suspect. Phillips Royce, for instance, will inherit some money. Probably a tidy sum."

Wilsher said, "There's no evidence of blood at the scene, except on the foyer floor, on the stairs, and in Favor's bed. Her head of course, too."

"We don't have a cause of death, yet," Robertson said. "At least not an official one."

"Nothing from Missy?" Branden asked.

"Working on it," Robertson said.

Niell said, "I think Jenny disliked Favor more than Sally did. Stands to reason, I guess."

"Why?" Robertson asked.

"She's protective," Niell said. "Of Sally. And as tough as she is, Sally has still cried a tear or two over this. There might be a wedge we could drive between the two."

Newell asked, "Is there any way to map the movements, or make a chronology of who was where? Maybe for the dinner party, or later last night?"

"There were people everywhere," Branden said. "Bar, kitchen, library. Plus the parlor and dining room, which you'd expect for a dinner party."

"Bliss isn't going to be any help," Robertson said. "Even if he were inclined to help, he was in and out, plowing a lot of the time. I don't think he even saw Favor retire."

Wilsher said, "I've still got men shoveling snow. Not going to find anything, is my guess now."

"We do know who left after the crowd, and in approximately what order," Branden said.

Robertson nodded, said, "But not only those left in the house can be regarded as suspects. Someone could have come back." He looked pointedly at Branden.

Branden wondered nervously when Wilsher's men would bring in the bloody clothes from Sonny Favor's car. As long as Martha was under Dr. Carson's care, Robertson would have to wait to learn anything more about Martha. Just a few more hours. Time to let Martha heal, he thought. Time to get her back to talking, before she faced the aggressive sheriff.

Wilsher said, "I doubt if we're going to get anything out of the three kids. Not if they're smart."

"It's Henry DiSalvo who'll prove to be the smart one," Robertson said.

"And Bliss," Branden said.

"I don't like him," Newell said. "Won't tell us anything about the family."

Robertson rocked forward in his chair and set his cup on the desk delicately. He took a pencil and began to tap the eraser end slowly on the rich cherry wood. "Ricky, you stay on Jenny for now," he said. "I'm guessing that DiSalvo will keep Sonny and Sally together for interviews. Mike, you can help with that."

Branden nodded, stood up, and hung his coat on a rack beside the door.

"Bobby," Robertson concluded, "you help Dan with the physical evidence. Find out what Missy has, as soon as she's got something. This case is going to boil down to that. The physical evidence. Because I doubt anyone is going to confess. The bloody clothes, first. And don't forget the green pitcher. I especially want to know about that."

Out in the hall, Niell took the professor aside and said, "Did you know Favor had affairs?"

Intrigued, Branden said simply, "Yes," and waited.

"With the art professor?"

"Her current," Branden said.

"With Dick Pomeroy?"

"There were rumors."

"How about with the president of your grand institution?"

"Arne Laughton?"

Niell nodded.

Branden arched an eyebrow.

"Then there's something more with Sonny Favor's girlfriend," Ricky said. "She evidently had it going on with your art professor, too."

25

Saturday, November 2
11:45 A.M.

SERGEANT Ricky Niell retrieved his uniform waistcoat from the peg in the sheriff's office and exited the jail through the main entrance in front of the Civil War monument on the snow-covered courthouse square. He circled the tall sandstone courthouse using the plowed sidewalks, and crossed Monroe Street, where the Favor limousine was still parked in spaces reserved for buggies. Several curious Amish lads had their hats off, pressing their faces to the tinted windows of the long vehicle. The worker in Carhartt coveralls was standing in slush at the curb, talking indignantly with the driver of a tow truck backed up to the rear bumper of the limo. Niell allowed himself only a wry smile on the outside, but inwardly enjoyed a head-back belly laugh. Without comment on the imminent towing operation, he bought a pack of cigarettes at the BP station and walked into the back entrance of the jail with a sense of satisfaction that almost troubled him.

Inside Interview A, he took off his coat, handed the cigarettes to Jenny Radcliffe, and sat down next to her, near the end of the gray metal table. She opened the pack immediately, lighted one for herself, and offered one to Ricky. He declined.

After a suitable pause, Ricky said, "I checked in the other room, Jenny. I got the impression Sally wants to see you."

"I'll go over there," Jenny said and started to rise.

Niell touched her forearm. "I'm afraid Sheriff Robertson won't allow that."

"What a pig!"

"It's Sally's lawyer, too, Jenny. He'll agree with that. You've got your own lawyers coming down from Wooster, not that you need them."

"I don't."

"Mr. DiSalvo will keep you separate. That's how he'll handle his responsibility to Sally and Sonny. He's their lawyer, not yours."

"If you told her that I wanted her in here with me, she'd come."

"I suppose it's worth a try," Ricky allowed, sympathetically. "I doubt Robertson would go for it, though."

"I need to see her," Jenny complained.

"It's too bad, too," Ricky said. "Sally is 'lawyered up' with her brother, and I'm not sure that's in her best interests."

Jenny looked puzzled.

"What if Sonny killed his mother?" Ricky explained. "That puts Sally at a disadvantage, having the same lawyer."

"Sally didn't do anything," Jenny said, and drew hard on her cigarette. "Could you try to get her to come in here and talk with me?"

"I'll try."

Jenny studied the glowing end of her cigarette intently and said, "You can't really think Sonny could have killed her."

"It's a possibility that we have to consider."

"He can be vicious. Vengeful and mean at times. Then he's also got his unassertive side. Kinda blows hot and cold."

"That's what I'm pointing out to you, Jenny. Robertson will be looking hard at Sonny Favor for this murder. So, you've got to ask yourself—Do you want Sally tied up with the same lawyer?"

Jenny stubbed out her cigarette. "Sonny has a blind spot where his mother is concerned. Down deep, he knows she never truly believed in him. She always had him figured as a failure ahead of time."

Ricky waited silently.

Jenny lighted another smoke and said, "Sally calls him the Eunuch. He could never stand up to their mother. And then, under the frustration of trying to please her, his moods would swing wild. I'm a psychology major, so I know all about this sort of thing. He's got a passive/aggressive thing going, and can't control it."

"Are you saying he is like his mother?" Ricky probed.

"In some ways. He uses money to control people. That's like her. Couldn't have gotten himself into a fraternity any other way. But he has no follow-through with people. Can't really commit."

"He does have a girlfriend, from what I understand."

"Maybe he does, and maybe he doesn't," Jenny said.

"Which means?"

"Sonny can't handle commitments. He thinks he's got a girlfriend, but that will change over the smallest thing. Sally says he's got an on/off switch in his mind. There's never any real heart involved in his relationships. His mind goes 'click,' and then he's done with someone forever. Absolutely done with them. You wouldn't ever want to be stuck in a crowded lifeboat with Sonny Favor."

"That doesn't sound very mature," Ricky said.

"Sally thinks he's damaged goods. Lost his father young, and his mother was the ice queen. He probably will never form a lasting attachment. Sad. So many men are screwed up like that. Sonny's also screwed up because his mother was more of a man-figure than he could ever be."

"I gather Sally didn't like that."

"I'm sure you know about last night," Jenny said. "Sally never backs down from her mother. Threw that thing at her from the mantel. Almost hit her, too."

"What thing?"

"A trophy thing. More of that useless male macho crap."

"Why do you think Sally did that?"

"Because Sonny was going to cave in to their mother's wishes when she threatened to block their trusts."

"So, Sonny did have motive for murder."

"Please. Sonny? Never his mother. Someone else, maybe, but never her. He couldn't say no to her, and he couldn't see who she really was. Couldn't understand what she had done to ruin him. Kill his mother? Not a chance in the world. He's the Eunuch."

"Evidently Mrs. Favor didn't castrate all her men," Ricky said.

Jenny looked puzzled again.

"Her affair with the art professor."

"Give me a break. Royce is a stumble-down drunk. She used him as a toy."

After a pause, Niell remarked, "Sally's got herself some kind of family."

"I need to talk to her."

"Robertson won't permit that."

"Why do you work for a creep like him?"

"Who, Robertson? He's not so bad."

"He's a throw-back. A twentieth-century dolt."

"His girlfriend doesn't think so."

"You're kidding."

"What?"

"He's got a girlfriend?"

"A very beautiful one. They'll probably get married."

"What in the world would a woman see in him?"

"What do you see in Sally?"

"She's genuine. Loving. Strong."

"So is Robertson."

"He's a pig!"

"No, Jenny. You're wrong on that one."

"He's a brute male slob."

"He's all man, if that's what you mean."

"Macho perversions."

"A year and a half ago, Robertson almost died pulling a deputy from a burning car. That's not macho. It's loyalty, bravery. It almost cost him his life, but he'd do it again tomorrow for any one of us."

"That's just what a woman needs," Jenny said sarcastically.

"If you took the time to know him, you'd find he's genuine. The most forthright man I know. You might even find you'd like him."

"I doubt that very seriously."

Ricky shrugged. "Dr. Melissa Taggert is also someone you'd like. A lot. And she's . . . "

"His girlfriend?"

"Right. Surprised?"

"She's a doctor?"

"Coroner."

"Seems like she could do better than Sheriff Robertson."

"Sheriff Robertson is not your enemy," Ricky said. "Somebody murdered Sally's mother, and I don't think it was you."

"It wasn't."

"I don't think it was Sally, either."

"It wasn't!"

"Then why is Sally 'lawyered up' in the next room without you?"

"Look, Sergeant Ricky, I want to talk to Sally. I don't want to say anything more until I talk to her."

Ricky gave the appearance of sincere thought. "I'll see what I can do."

26

WHILE Martha slept upstairs, Pastor Cal Troyer arrived at the Brandens' home and took a seat in the living room with Caroline and Evelyn. After discussing Martha's present troubles, he said, "I've counseled with her several times. She sometimes stays late after a Wednesday night service."

"Can you tell us what about?" Caroline asked.

"Personal things," Cal said, averting his eyes.

Evelyn said, "There are some unresolved issues stemming from her sessions with me."

"She hasn't spoken to either of you all morning?" Cal asked.

Evelyn said, "She was pretty out of it when I found her this morning. We're afraid the blood has something to do with the murder of Juliet Favor."

"Good grief," Cal said, shaking his head. "Martha is not capable of anything like that."

"If you're referring to the fact that she is Mennonite," Evelyn said, "let me assure you, as deep as her troubles likely are, we have to consider it at least possible that she's involved in some way."

"She's not just Mennonite," Cal explained. "She's conservative Mennonite. What some people call 'country' Mennonite."

"OK," Evelyn said tentatively. "I just think you ought to know I've seen quite a lot in my practice, Amish and Mennonite."

Cal nodded. "Her congregation—well, her parents' congregation, anyway—is led by Ben Mast. He used to be Black Bumper Amish. Came out of an Old Order sect that decided to buy cars, so long as they were painted to be plain. No shiny metal. As significant as the transition was, the sect still will not permit violence of any kind. Mennonites are pacifists. It just doesn't figure."

Evelyn held firm. "I wouldn't argue with you on that point, Cal. I just know how much she's been hurt. How many issues she still faces. And what I see in her today—well, this is a young woman in extreme crisis. Something has got a hold of her deep down, and if it's what I think, she may have been capable of almost anything. Rage, violence, even suicide."

Cal shook his head from side to side, rubbing his short white beard with the gnarled fingers of his carpenter's hands.

Evelyn asked, "What did you talk about with her, Cal?"

"Personal problems, all confidential, I'm afraid. Lifestyle issues for the most part."

Caroline asked, "Has she been seeing anyone other than Sonny Favor?"

Said Cal, "He's pretty much the one. You say she's sleeping now?"

"Upstairs," Caroline said.

"From what I know of Sonny Favor," Cal said, as he left, "you're gonna want to be here when she wakes up."

IN THE Brandens' living room, Evelyn and Caroline became only slowly aware of the drop in temperature. They had sat talking quietly, watching the snow falling heavily again outside the big living room windows at the front of the house, and the house had grown colder incrementally, to the point where they noticed it only now.

Caroline got up and followed a draft into the kitchen and then the family room. There, she found the sliding door open, and she closed it. She motioned to Evelyn, and the two climbed the stairs together, finding the covers folded back on Martha's bed, and no Martha. The phone that normally sat on the nightstand had been pulled over to the bed, and it sat there, line stretched across the sheet.

Back downstairs, they went out onto the back porch through the sliding door and found the storm door at the steps ajar. In the new snow outside on the steps, there were fresh footprints, made by small, flat shoes, and the tracks angled across the backyard to the cliffs at the edge of the lot.

Caroline ran out into the snow without her coat. She reached the edge of the cliffs swiftly, and Evelyn saw her stop there and peer over. She saw Caroline cup her hands to her mouth, and shout over the edge. The snow muffled the sound of her voice, but Evelyn heard, "Martha! Martha!" before Caroline turned back from the line of barren trees.

Once inside, Caroline kicked off her shoes and started lacing on winter boots. Evelyn said, "Caroline," softly.

Pushing her arms into her coat sleeves, Caroline said, "She's gone down that steep path. Can't see through the snow, but I can catch her, I know I can, Evelyn."

Dr. Carson took Caroline gently by the shoulders and said, "Bringing her back here isn't going to help."

"What are you talking about?"

"Martha has some decisions to make, Caroline. Even if you could catch her, that wouldn't change anything."

"She's not fit to go off on her own."

"She's stronger than you think."

Relenting, Caroline took off her coat and laid it on the couch.

"She's going to have to make some important choices, soon," Evelyn added.

Said Caroline, "I wanted to help her."

"We still can. When she comes to us. Then it will count for something. Until now, we were just watching her, anyway."

"What about her baby?"

"What could you tell her now?"

"What about her boyfriend?"

"She has to decide."

Caroline sat down heavily, arms limp at her sides. Her stocking feet were cold and wet from the snow. "I know what you've said about John Schlabaugh, but I don't think I can handle it if she goes back to him."

"If she has, it ought to be obvious when we talk to him tomorrow," Evelyn said.

"The phone," Caroline said, and started off for the bedroom.

There she sat on the edge of the bed, dialed *69, and got an answer, "I told you I can't talk, Martha."

"Who is this?" Caroline inquired.

"Sonny Favor. I'm busy."

"Did you talk recently to Martha?"

"Who is this?"

"Mrs. Michael Branden."

"Oh. Mrs. Branden. Your husband is right here."

"Sonny, I need to know if you talked with Martha. I know she called this number."

"What if I did?"

"You did, didn't you. She's left, Sonny, and we need to find her."

"I can't help you, Mrs. Branden."

"Sonny, it's important. I'm sorry about your mother, but I need to find Martha, now."

"I'll let you talk to Dr. Branden," he said, and handed the phone across the table in the jail's Interview B. "It's your wife," he said to the professor.

"Caroline, something wrong?"

"Martha left. Hiked down over the cliffs while we were talking with Cal Troyer in the living room."

"I see," Branden said. Robertson and the whole Favor entourage were in the room, their eyes focused on him.

"You can't talk?" Caroline asked.

"No."

"Did Sonny take a call a little before this one?"

"Yes."

"It was Martha."

"OK."

"Did you hear his end of the conversation?"

"Yes. I'll call you back."

When she hung up, Caroline said to Evelyn Carson, "Martha called Sonny Favor. At least we know she's talking now."

27

Saturday, November 2
Noon

BRUCE Robertson stood at the end of the table in Interview B and watched the professor's expression as he handed the cell phone back across the table to Sonny Favor. Clearly, the professor wasn't happy. And clearly, he had not wanted to talk in front of people.

And this was the second call to that phone in the last ten minutes, the sheriff mused. In the first call, Sonny had evidently been talking to Martha Lehman. He had said Martha several times, once not politely. Judging from the one end of the conversation he had heard, Robertson surmised that things had started off pleasantly enough, and then had turned convincingly adversarial, as if Sonny had switched to talking to someone new and foreign. Last of all, the boy had curtly said, "I can't deal with that, now. You're going to have to take care of that problem on your own."

After switching off, Sonny had been quiet and sullen, but the second call had seemed to fluster him again. He took the phone back from Branden, pocketed it, stood up, and said, "I don't want to be here anymore."

Robertson said, "We still have questions, Mr. Favor, about last night."

Sonny looked down at DiSalvo, seated next to Branden, and said, "Do I have to stay?" His cheeks were vibrant red, and his eyes focused intensely on his lawyer, as he rocked in place from one foot to the other. He seemed to Robertson to be about ready to bolt from the room.

DiSalvo said, "I think we've talked long enough, Sheriff. The kids have nothing more to add."

"They have not cooperated with our investigation, Henry. I take note of that."

"I beg to differ," DiSalvo said. "They've each accounted for their actions. We have nothing more to add here."

DiSalvo rose. Sally stood up when DiSalvo held her chair, and the three navigated their way to the door. Out in the hall, DiSalvo held out his card for Robertson.

"I don't need your dang card, Henry!" Robertson barked. "What in the world's the matter with you, anyways?"

"I'm their lawyer, Bruce, at least for now. A new fellow is flying in from New York City. Ought to be here by this evening. Until then, the children have nothing more they can tell you under my instructions."

With that, Henry DiSalvo, longtime friend to Robertson, Branden, and everyone else in the sheriff's office, turned curtly and led his charges out the front door of the jail. That left Robertson and Branden standing alone in the pine-paneled hallway. Robertson read anxiety on Branden's face and guessed it had to do with Martha Lehman.

Said Robertson, "I think you'd better bring Martha Lehman in to see me."

"OK, Bruce, but we've got a problem."

"She's Sonny girlfriend, there's the blood, and she left his house driving his car last night."

"There's more."

"Give, Mike. Right now."

"You know Evelyn Carson has been taking care of Martha Lehman since she found her outside her office early this morning."

"Like you said earlier."

"And that Martha was mute, again."

"That was Martha talking on the phone with Sonny just now?"

"Right. But now she's missing."

"What do you mean, missing? I thought she was with Carson."

"Caroline and Evelyn drove her over to my house to rest, and she took off when they thought she was asleep."

"Blood on her clothes, and now you've lost her, Mike. That just tears it."

"We won't know it's Juliet Favor's blood until we have it tested."

"'We' aren't going to be testing anything, Professor."

"Dan Wilsher has the clothes, Bruce. Missy can test them any time she wants."

"I don't want you having anything more to do with Martha Lehman, Mike. Not a damn thing."

"I couldn't know she'd skip out like this," Branden complained, gesturing haplessly.

"Yeah, well, now she's gone. I ought to run the three of you in."

"Evelyn's got a right to treat her patient. To protect her while she's vulnerable."

"I still ought to run you and Caroline in. You for withholding evidence! Caroline for harboring a material witness!"

"If we had brought Martha right out to the Favor mansion this morning, at the earliest possible moment, what would you have done?"

"I'd have asked her about the blood on her clothes."

"You're not hearing me. She wasn't talking. She was in shock. You couldn't have gotten a thing from her."

"At least she'd be in custody."

Branden sighed. "This was just a couple of hours ago, Bruce. We needed time to bring Martha out of a stupor. Time to see what we were up against at the Favor house. And just as soon as I knew we couldn't produce Martha on demand, I told you about it. So cut me some slack, OK?"

"I don't want you talking to Martha Lehman, Mike. You're to stay out of that part of this case."

"OK."

"I mean it, Mike."

"I heard you."

"Geez All Mighty, Mike."

"We'll find her."

"No, you won't. My people are gonna do that. You're gonna stay the hell out of it. You can handle the college people for background, but that's it."

Branden studied the sheriff's eyes and saw raw determination there, mixed with anger. He ruffled his brown hair and said, "All right, Bruce."

"Nothing whatsoever to do with Martha Lehman," Bruce said with emphasis.

"All right," Branden said, allowing some exasperation to sound in his voice.

"And you'll let me know what you find out about the college people who were at dinner last night."

"Right," Branden said, sounding distracted.

"Maybe you'd better just stay out of the case altogether."

"No, look. I can still be of some help."

"What do you propose to do?" Robertson asked.

"I need to call Caroline," Branden said, and turned into the empty squad room.

Alone in the hall, Robertson allowed his mind to wander over aspects of the case. The blood on Martha Lehman's clothes was a bombshell. And Martha had driven Sonny's car back out to the Favor residence early that morning, when Juliet Favor had evidently been killed. Other aspects of the case seemed less important, but Robertson knew not to disengage from them now. It was a tangled ball of string, when taken whole. The problem was, there were a hundred loose ends in this ball of string. None as prominent as bloody clothes, but that would have to wait for Missy Taggert's analysis before it meant anything solid in this case. But, in addition to the Martha Lehman string, there was the Sonny/Sally string, tied to a motive of inheritance? Or maybe just kids hating their mother. The dinner party string, tied to a couple dozen motives, all having to do with the financial reorganizations Juliet Favor had been poised to institute? Branden, who knew the players better than anyone, was the key to unraveling that tangled mess. There was also the physical evidence. That might prove to be the most promising. Dan Wilsher's search of the house and grounds. Bobby Newell's green pitcher and the other items at the scene. Which connected, Robertson thought, to Missy Taggert—crime scene analysis and the actual, official cause of death.

Robertson walked back into his large, paneled office and dialed the morgue in the basement of Joel Pomerene Memorial Hospital. After two rings, he heard Melissa Taggert answer, "Taggert."

"Hi, Missy. Do you have any bloody clothes to test?"

"Don't know anything about that."

"One of Mike's students turned up at Evelyn Carson's office this morning with blood on her clothes."

"Nothing like that here, Bruce."

"Have you heard from Dan Wilsher?"

"No. Should I have?"

"According to Mike Branden, he'll be bringing in clothes with blood samples to test."

"Don't have them yet."

"Then I'll have Ellie get him on the radio."

"OK, but whose clothes are they?"

"Belong to Sonny Favor's girlfriend."

"Good grief, Bruce."

"I know. Mike screwed up."

"You'll have to explain that one to me."

Robertson gave her a brief rundown and said, "She's been in no shape to talk, anyways, but now she's also missing."

"What's that mean?"

"Caroline Branden and Evelyn Carson were taking care of her. First they couldn't get her to talk and now she's skipped out, and they don't know where she is."

"Evelyn Carson will do what's best for her patient, Bruce."

"I know that. But Mike could have brought her in sooner."

"If she needed to be in the care of a psychiatrist, then Mike probably couldn't have done that. Carson would be calling the shots, not him."

"Mike doesn't believe this girl could have killed Juliet Favor."

"Why?"

"She's Mennonite."

"Then I'd have to agree with Mike."

"I backed him off the case a bit."

"I don't have to tell you how much you can trust Mike Branden."

"I just don't like the idea of him staying involved with the Martha Lehman aspects of the case."

"OK. Are you still coming for lunch?"

"I thought we could go home and grab something there."

"It's a working lunch, Bruce. I told you it'd be that way this morning. There's too much that doesn't make sense about Juliet Favor. You can bring something from home."

Robertson grimaced. "I can't eat lunch if you're gonna be cutting something, Missy."

"All the cutting is done, Sweetheart. Now, it's just samples, instruments, and analysis."

"If you promise," the sheriff said. "Are you going to be able to finish by tonight?"

"What time's our flight tomorrow?"

"Nine-thirty."

"I'll get enough done for now. Have you told anyone we're leaving?"

"I told Ellie," Branden said. "I'll tell Bobby and Dan later this afternoon."

"Are you sure we have to go?"

"Like I said, Babe, I've got plans."

HALF an hour later, Sheriff Robertson lumbered into the basement labs at the hospital with tuna fish sandwiches and a thermos of coffee. Coroner Taggert was seated at her desk in the little office off the larger lab, draped in a white lab coat. When she saw the chaotic sheriff, she instinctively closed several manila folders that she had open on her desk, and slipped them safely into a drawer. As she rose to wriggle out of her lab coat, Robertson put the thermos and brown paper sack on the desktop, and slipped a big arm around her back, underneath the lab coat, trapping her arms behind her back. He leaned her backward and kissed her, first on the lips and then on the ear and neck. She laughed, struggled free, and said, "Bruce!" nervous to see if anyone had observed them. Her lab tecs had gone to lunch themselves, so she relaxed, took her lab coat off the rest of the way, and snuggled up to the front of him. They kissed again, and he whispered in her ear.

"Not here," Missy said, laughing. She pushed the big sheriff away. He stepped back to her, wrapped his arms around her at the waist, and lifted her off her feet as if she were a paper doll. He twirled once in place, and sat Missy down on the desk, kissing her again.

"Bruce, we can't," Missy protested, blushing.

"Can't help it, Babe, seeing you in your lab coat like that."

"What?"

"Your lab coat, Missy. Drives me nuts."

Her eyes sparkled. "I'll wear it home someday."

"Tonight."

"Bruce!"

"Tonight, or you're not getting off this desk."

"If I wear this coat home, it's going to be all I wear."

"Promises, promises," Robertson said, smiling. He eased back from her and pulled her off the desk. "It's been a hard morning, Babe. Got a thousand suspects, and no hard facts."

Missy smoothed out the front of her pink blouse and black wool skirt. "I don't exactly have much to help you here, I'm afraid."

Robertson picked up a stack of graphs of some kind, 8.5 x 11 sheets stapled together, and started turning the pages.

"No you don't, Big Guy," Missy said, and took the pages back. By the time she had those safely tucked into a drawer, Robertson had taken two or three microscope slides off her desk, and was holding one up to the ceiling light. She reached up, lifted it out of his fingers and held out her hands for the others. "Hand them over, Sheriff," she ordered.

Robertson smiled and shrugged. "Just trying to help," he said.

"I need your help in here like I need a hole in the head."

"People say you've already got a few holes in your head, engaged to me."

"Oh? Are we engaged now? Who told me?"

"I thought we might give that a try."

"Give it a try? Sounds sooo romantic."

"Ah, Missy. You know what I mean."

"If you're going to propose to me, Bruce Robertson, it had better be the most seriously romantic thing you've ever done in your entire life."

"It's like that, is it?"

"It is. Now, where's my lunch?"

Robertson eyed the beautiful coroner for a long twenty seconds and considered the weight of what he had just heard. Done properly, it seemed, Missy Taggert had just given him better than half a chance of proposing successfully. "The most seriously romantic thing," he repeated in his mind. He froze with a hundred amazing thoughts, and he seemed to lose his place in the world for a moment. He had held the idea out to her as a single impulsive rose, and she had transformed it to a dozen arbors in full summer bloom.

Nuances were sometimes lost on Sheriff Bruce Robertson, but this one he got. He knew in that brief exchange that their relationship had transcended itself. They were to be engaged. He was to do it right. He gazed into her eyes and made a silent covenant with his heart.

For her part, Missy noted the reverence that had passed over his eyes, and she said, "Tuna fish, Bruce?" When his eyes were focused again, she was lifting the sandwiches out of their brown paper bag.

"Best I could do," he said.

"It'll be fine."

Robertson sat down beside her desk and ate quietly, watching her eyes. She ate quietly, too. When they were finished, she stood up and walked into the lab, where Mrs. Favor lay under a white cover, head tilted to the left, the gash at the back of her skull lighted from above. Robertson came alongside, and Missy said, "She took a tremendous blow to the back of her head, here. A really vicious blow."

Robertson leaned over to study the wound.

"Bone fragments from the skull penetrated the brain, but that didn't kill her," Missy said.

"There should have been a lot of blood, but we can't find any out at the house," Robertson said.

"There wouldn't have been much," Missy said. "Everything says she was already dead when she got clobbered."

"Are you sure?"

"County pays me to be."

"Then how did she die?"

"I don't know, yet. The tox screens are negative, at least at this preliminary stage."

"We were going to have you test a green pitcher and the contents of several sink traps."

"I already did that. Those were the papers you rifled on my desk." She retrieved them. "These are GC/MS plots for all the water samples. There is nothing out of the ordinary in them."

"I thought that was going to be a good angle."

"All I found was low levels of pesticide residue and the things you normally expect in well water. You might want to tell the family to drill a better well. This one is marginal."

"No poisons? Sedatives?"

"Just water, Bruce, plus the trace contaminants everybody has in their wells. I'm afraid pure water samples are hard to come by, these days."

"I think she hit her head on the foyer floor. You say it cracked her skull?"

"Something did."

"Then how'd she get back upstairs?"

"She didn't move herself anywhere, after this injury, Bruce. Aside from the fact that she was already dead, it would have been instantly fatal."

"Somebody moved her, then."

"Trouble with that is, she didn't lose much blood at all, wherever she was killed. Her blood volumes are right where they should be. Remember, the head wound didn't kill her."

"We thought that maybe she was drugged before she died."

Taggert stepped to the bench along the back wall and held up a small bottle with a ground-glass stopper. "I thought of that, too. This is DMSO." She pointed out the label on the bottle.

"And that is?"

"It's a solvent, for one thing, but it's also known for its ability to penetrate skin. From what I understand, she used this for migraine headaches."

"How's that fit with poisoning?"

"You could put a sedative in the DMSO, and it would go into the skin right along with the solvent."

"You found no poison in it?"

"Just DMSO and water. It's unusual to mix it with water, but that's all it is—water."

There was a knock, and they turned to see Captain Dan Wilsher rapping his knuckles on the metal frame of the door to the lab. He carried in a brown plastic garbage bag and set it on the floor next to the coroner's autopsy table. As he took off coat and gloves, he said, "We haven't found any bloody rags or clothes at the Favor residence, Bruce, inside or out." To Missy, he greeted, "Coroner."

"Captain," Missy said and nodded at the garbage bag.

"Right," Wilsher said. "You'll want some gloves and tongs or something."

Missy snapped into a pair of examination gloves and took a large pair of forceps out of a drawer. She set the garbage bag on its side, on the table at Favor's feet, and teased the opening wide with the forceps. Reaching inside, she clamped down on fabric and drew out a long, green skirt, heavily wrinkled. Next came out a pair of black panty hose and a white lace prayer cap with long string ties. There was also a pink blouse. From the bottom of the bag, Melissa pulled out a white apron crusted in the middle with a moderate amount of dried blood.

"This all came out of the trunk of Sonny Favor's Lexus," Wilsher said.

28

Saturday, November 2
12:30 P.M.

WHILE Missy sorted through the clothes a second time, Robertson
returned to her desk and dialed the jail. "Ellie," he said. "Is Mike
Branden still there? OK. Tell him to stay put. What? You're kidding. Who did that? No. No. Right, that's a parking violation, so
there's a fine. Plus the towing fee. Doesn't matter. Once Ed Lorentz
hooks onto your bumper, that's a towing fee whether he moves it
five miles or five feet."

When the sheriff entered the jail by the back door, there was
pandemonium at the far end of the hall, where Ellie Troyer-Niell
stood defensively behind her counter, shaking her head emphati-
cally as Henry DiSalvo held out a check. When the sheriff reached
her, Ellie was saying, "You have to pay those fines at the courthouse."

Robertson said to DiSalvo, "What's going on, Henry?"

DiSalvo said, "Ed Lorentz won't release the Favor limousine until
we've paid our fines, and the courthouse isn't open for business on
Saturdays."

Daniel Bliss, behind DiSalvo, stepped forward and began, "Now,
see here, Sheriff."

Robertson cut him off. "Just hold on there, Bliss." To Ellie he
said, "What's the total?"

Ed Lorentz piped up from near the front door. "My fee is $150,
and that's final!"

"Really," Bliss turned and said. "I doubt your whole truck is worth that much."

Lorentz said, "Oh, yeah?" and took a step forward. Robertson came out from behind the counter.

"Oh, please!" Bliss said to the approaching Lorentz, and raised his hands in disgust.

Bliss stood next to DiSalvo. Sonny Favor stood back from the counter, holding himself apart from the fracas. Sally and Jenny held hands near the Pepsi machine, and a new man in a suit stood next to them. Branden was leaning on an elbow at Ellie's counter, Ricky Niell to his left. Robertson took a position between Ed Lorentz and Daniel Bliss. Instantly, everyone was shouting, and just as instantly, Ellie put two fingers between her teeth and gave out an ear-shattering whistle that brought the whole crowd to silence. Forcefully, she said, "I'm not a cashier, so you all clear on out of my lobby!"

Robertson's grin went ear-to-ear. DiSalvo quietly slipped his check into the vest pocket of his three-piece suit. Daniel Bliss threw his hands in the air, to the great entertainment of Ed Lorentz.

"My office, everyone, now," Robertson ordered. Once they were all packed into his office, Robertson said, "Ed, will you take their check?"

"Cash only!" Lorentz intoned.

"Oh, my God!" Bliss said and took out his wallet. He counted out bills, held them out stiffly to Lorentz, and turned his back once Lorentz had taken the payment.

The man in the suit stepped forward and laid his card on the sheriff's desk. "I'm John Lumbaird, Miss Radcliffe's lawyer."

Robertson ignored the man.

DiSalvo said, "We'll be leaving now," and led out the door. Sonny followed first, and then the rest, leaving Professor Branden beside the credenza, where he poured a cup of coffee and smiled to the point of outright laughter.

"Oh, you think this is funny?" Robertson barked and sat down behind his desk.

Branden shrugged and stirred creamer into his coffee. A silence ensued, during which Branden sprawled in his usual place, a low leather chair in front of Robertson's desk. The sheriff studied the card left by Jenny Radcliffe's lawyer. To Branden, he said, "Anything about Martha yet?"

Branden frowned, shook his head, stood up, and moved to the windows facing west onto Clay Street. Heavy snow fell in large, soft flakes as traffic splashed through the slush on the pavement. Branden thought about the fresh tracks in the snow that Caroline had described when he had called her from the empty squad room. So, Martha had called Sonny. They knew that from the *69 callback. But, had she mentioned her pregnancy? That did fit Sonny's reaction. "You'll have to take care of that on your own," he had said. No wonder she ran away. But, to where? Or to whom? Could Sonny Favor cut and run from a relationship, just like that? Probably. Branden knew the boy as well as anyone did, short of his doctors and family. It was the bloody apron, though, that seemed to register most with Robertson. And why not? Nothing else struck bone like that. Not in this case. Two dozen suspects, an equal number of motives, and Martha Lehman coming to her senses, and doing what? Running.

Ricky Niell came into the room and sat down in front of Robertson's desk.

"I really don't know where she is, Bruce," Branden said, turning from the snowfall outside. "If I did, I'd bring her in myself."

"Not if you thought she killed Favor."

"You don't think she did that, any more than I do, Bruce. At most, she'll serve as a material witness. Testify as to what she saw."

"I want her, Mike. Like a Dade County Democrat wants a recount."

"I can't produce her. I'm getting tired of telling you that."

Robertson threw up his hands and leaned his swivel-rocker back as far as it would go. He stared up at the ornate squares of the hand-hammered tin ceiling tiles and said, "Missy doesn't think the blow to the head is what killed Favor. Says she was dead some time before she got hit in the head."

Branden's attention soared. "Then all the bloody apron tells us is that she was there after Favor was killed."

"It doesn't tell us where your Martha was before or during the murder," Robertson said. "But, I don't get it. What's that crack in the marble floor, anyways?"

"Now you're coming around to my way of thinking," Branden said.

"Then we really don't know how she was killed," Niell said.

"We're nowhere in this case, Bruce," Branden said.

"How could Mrs. Favor die first, and then haul herself upstairs?" Niell asked.

"She couldn't," Robertson said, frustrated. He reached instinctively for a pack of cigarettes in his shirt pocket, and cursed aloud.

"So, that means Martha's apron doesn't necessarily tie her to a murder," Branden said after a moment.

"At the very least," Robertson said, "it ties her to a dead body. Providing the blood matches."

Branden shook his head sadly. "She found her, Bruce. Cleaned her up and cleared out, nothing more."

Niell said, "So, who killed her, and how?"

Robertson tilted his chair back level. "Back to square one," he said.

"OK," Branden said. "Maybe Martha went back to see her, much later that night."

"Why?" Robertson asked.

Niell said, "Mrs. Favor bawled her out. Called her cheap trash. Maybe Martha went back to confront her."

"At 5:00 A.M.?" Robertson asked.

"Or, maybe she went back for Sonny," Niell proposed.

Branden privately thought that was as plausible as anything he had heard, but he said, "She might have gone back to talk to his mother."

"This is all conjecture," Bruce complained. "The whole thing runs in circles."

"It explains how she got blood on her apron," Niell said.

"We can't even be sure how Juliet Favor died," Robertson said.

"What did Missy tell you, exactly, Bruce?" Branden asked.

"The blow to her head was delivered *post mortem*. There were no toxins in her system. The green pitcher and sink traps held water only. Well water to be specific. The little medicine bottle held DMS something."

"DMSO," Branden said. "She rubbed that on her temples for headaches."

"You know about that?" Robertson asked.

"Dick Pomeroy told me. It goes right into the skin."

"Could have been a sedative or something mixed in with that," Niell offered.

"Missy checked," Robertson said, shaking his head. "It was just DMSO and water."

"Is she sure?" Branden asked. "Is her test reliable?"

"For the most part. She did that GC test and had a bunch of graphs. But all the bottle held was DMSO, plus water. Even had the same trace impurities as drinking water."

Branden frowned. "Missy can't find a cause of death?"

"Not at this point," Robertson said. "When I left her, she was planning on a more complete autopsy. Gonna send samples out, that sort of thing."

"Good grief," Branden said, rubbing his temples. "It could have been anyone."

"Or more than one," Niell said. "I mean, one person to kill her, however that was done, plus another to clunk her in the head, after she was dead."

"Clunk her with what?" Robertson asked.

"Then Martha came on the scene last," Branden said. "That ex-onerates her."

"Clunk her with what?" Robertson repeated.

Niell shrugged and said, "Also, when?"

Robertson unwrapped a stick of gum and popped it into his mouth.

Branden blinked double and stared at the sheriff. He looked around the room, studied Robertson's desktop, and shook his head. Incredulously, the professor said, "You're not smoking!"

Robertson smiled. "Wondered who'd be the first to notice."

Niell whistled. "It has been some kind of day."

"Is it Missy who has finally gotten you doing this?" Branden asked.

"Sort of," Robertson said.

"Way to go, Missy," Branden said.

Niell gave a thumbs-up.

"You don't seem unusually grouchy or impatient," Branden said.

"I'm not, dammit!" Robertson growled. "I'm on the patch." He rubbed the outside of his left arm, where the patch lay under his sleeve.

Branden whistled a low, respectful note.

"Anyway," Robertson said, "this isn't about me. I want to talk to Martha Lehman."

"Bruce, we all do," Branden said.

"If what you propose is true, she was the last person in the bed-room before Sonny found her dead this morning."

"And the trouble with that," Branden said, "is anyone could have killed her. Anyone could have hit her over the head. Might have been the same person, might not."

"That's not the biggest problem we have," Robertson said.

"Right," Niell agreed. "We still don't know how she was killed, let alone when, or by whom."

29

AFTER lunch Saturday, Professor Branden followed a salt truck heading west on Route 39. Near the high school, the truck swung out and around a buggy struggling through the deep snow, and Branden did, too. In the rear of the buggy, four small children in denim coats looked out the back opening of the rig, studying Branden's car, and waved shyly as he passed. As he came around into his lane, Branden glanced in the rearview mirror and saw stern Amish parents bundled in black wool coats, with a heavy blue blanket pulled up over their knees. The father had on a black felt hat with broad brim and round dome, and the missus wore a black bonnet tied closely against her cheeks.

The professor pulled into the drive of the Favor residence, and the buggy clattered by on the wet pavement behind him. At the front door, the deputy on guard took down the yellow crime scene ribbon, and Branden went inside. Once he had his coat off, he walked slowly through the house. He studied the layout for about twenty minutes and then heard a commotion at the front door. Returning to the foyer, Branden found Henry DiSalvo arguing with the deputy about access to the house. DiSalvo saw Branden and said, "Mike, let me in. The Favor children want some clothes."

Branden signaled the deputy to admit the lawyer and said to DiSalvo, "You can't take anything, Henry. You know that."

"They've all taken rooms at the Hotel Millersburg. They don't have a change of clothes or overnight bags. Thought I could at least pick up a few things for them," DiSalvo said. He draped his coat over an armchair and followed Branden into the parlor.

"You're not staying with the Favors?" Branden asked.

"Their New York lawyer is finally here. Landed a Lear jet at the Wayne County airport," Henry said. "It's a good thing, too, because I am completely worn out."

"I wondered how you were holding up, Henry."

"Criminal law is too much pressure. I like estate practice. Trusts, wills, that type of thing."

Branden had dealt with DiSalvo a year and a half ago, on an Amish inheritance of several million dollars. And DiSalvo had managed Branden's trust after his parents had been killed in a car accident involving a buggy when he was a boy.

"Even if it is just trusts and wills, Henry, I imagine the Favor account is enough to keep ten lawyers busy."

"Oh, I manage. I've been working for Juliet Favor since before her husband died," DiSalvo said, and took a seat on the yellow-flowered divan.

"I suppose you can't talk about their inheritance," Branden said, and stood by the cold fireplace. "Is this the rugby trophy Sally threw at her mother?" he asked.

DiSalvo said, "Yes," and rose. At the mantel, he took the brass figure of men tangled in a scrummage, and turned it around to face the other way. "Guess I put it up backwards," he remarked.

"How would you know?" Branden asked.

"I've got a duplicate in my office."

"I thought it looked familiar."

"Yep. Harry Favor was captain one year when I was coach. I'd started my practice in Millersburg, and I served as rugby coach at the college for several years."

"You've known the family a long time, Henry."

"I knew Juliet and Harry when they were just kids. Juliet was a poor Tennessee mountain girl, come to the big college up north.

Harry was a senior her freshman year. He fell in love with her the first day he saw her. They were married the day after she graduated."

"Big romance?"

"Star-crossed lovers, actually. His family was wealthy. Big upper East Coast types. Didn't approve much of plain Juliet Johnson."

"That's ironic."

"How so?"

"Juliet evidently had the same objection to Martha Lehman."

"Right," DiSalvo said, contemplatively. "One forgets one's roots."

"Or tries to," Branden said. "How much are these two kids worth, now?"

"In the neighborhood of 100 million dollars."

"Whew!" Branden said.

"That's 100 million each, conservatively. There's also a trifle, something like eight or nine million, provided for the college."

Branden shook his head. "Sonny said it was something like that." Putting a college kid together with that kind of money was something his mind resisted. He wondered, momentarily, how nine million would work out for the college. "Juliet was going to cut them off?" he asked.

"She only threatened to," DiSalvo said, "and then, only to a certain extent. But you already know that."

Branden took a seat in an armchair next to the fireplace, and DiSalvo returned to the divan. Branden mused, "That's a powerful motive for murder, Henry."

"You'd think so," Henry said. "But Sally never really cared about money. Just wanted a normal mother to love her. So, they fought all the time."

"And Sonny?"

"Juliet explained to him last night that she intended to change the will. Sally would get a fourth in cash, Sonny half, and Millersburg College the last fourth, but Sonny would have to jump through hoops to get his. It was the same in the trust his father had left him.

159

The same on three counts, actually—whether he got his trust or in-
herited through the old or the new will. He just learned about that
last night."

"What kind of hoops?"

"School, MBA, that type of thing. Juliet explained it all to him.
Whether through his trust, activated when he reached twenty-one,
or through an inheritance whenever Juliet died, Sonny Favor was
on the treadmill for the rest of his life."

"Not Sally too?"

"No, and I don't know why. Sally just gets her share in a lump
sum, one time. Sonny gets the true wealth—companies, holdings,
properties, directorships, etc., but he has to toe the line for it. And
Juliet laid that all out for him last night."

"That's an awful lot of money for a kid like Sonny to handle,"
Branden said.

"She knew that. So, she was all set to sell off a dozen companies
or so. Simplify the estate for him. He'd keep the simple manufac-
turing concerns, but high-technology companies like pharmaceuticals and computer chips were set to go."

"And it's still worth 100 million to him?"

"That's just the current valuation. Properly managed, the whole
thing could double itself in ten years, even in this market. Juliet
knew Sonny would have to measure up to pull that off, but she
thought it was a good carrot, so to speak."

"Why are you telling me all this, Henry?" Branden asked.

"Their new lawyer thought I should," Henry said. "Wants it
known to Sheriff Robertson that neither Sally nor Sonny had a real
motive to kill Juliet Favor."

"I guess not," Branden said.

Henry DiSalvo excused himself and left, and the fireplace drew
the professor's attention again. He thought of Sonny and Sally at
the Hotel Millersburg, working out their futures with their lawyers.
Amazing, the amounts involved, he thought. Branden tried to imagine the impact that that amount of money would have. Even for

children accustomed to great wealth, to be handed so vast a fortune while still in college would have to be astounding. The pressure, decisions, weight of it all—absolutely astounding.

Branden rose slowly from his chair and faced the fireplace, with his hands behind his back. Heavy snow continued to fall outside, and the room was cold. He retrieved his coat, turned to go, and then abruptly spun back to face the mantel.

In the foyer, he took out his cell phone and called Melissa Taggert. In a few urgent sentences, he explained why he needed a technician with a fingerprint kit, and why he would be sending said technician back to Missy's labs with a blood sample to test.

30

Saturday, November 2
6:20 P.M.

PROFESSOR Branden sat in front of the Saturday evening news so absorbed in his thoughts that he did not hear the weather treatise on the important patterns in "winds aloft." His eyes were directed at the TV, but his mind held his attention elsewhere. He missed the overnight forecast for another eight inches of snow.

Caroline Branden sat next to him on the couch in the family room. She noticed the distant focus in her husband's eyes, and reached across his lap to hit the remote button, turning off the set. The professor's expression did not change. She let him drift in his reverie for nearly ten minutes and then nudged his elbow. No effect. She nudged again, harder, and he turned to her and blinked.

"Tell me again about the trophy," she said.

Branden stirred and rubbed at the back of his neck. He saw that the television was off and asked, "News over?"

"I just turned it off." She smiled and rose to clear coffee cups from the end tables. Standing in front of him, poised to carry the dishes into the kitchen, she tipped her head that way and said, "Come tell me about the trophy again."

As she washed and he dried at the kitchen sink, the professor explained his deductions to her again, saying, "I wouldn't have noticed it at all if Henry hadn't turned it around to face the right way."

"One would think a backwards trophy would be easy to spot," Caroline said.

"It's a stylized brass replica of men crouched in a low rugby formation," he said. "You can turn it either way, and it wouldn't look wrong."

"So, how did Henry know the right way?"

"He was coach the year Harry Favor's team won the championship. Has a twin to that trophy in his office. Might be the only person in the world who'd have known it was backwards."

"So somebody like a maid just put it up wrong?" Caroline offered.

"Right," the professor said. "Except for the fact that Henry himself was the last person supposed to have touched it, Friday evening before Juliet Favor's dinner. He would have put it back on the mantel correctly."

"What does that tell us?"

"I think it's the key element to a number of facts in this case. Favor's crushed skull, and a crack in the marble floor. Martha's bloody apron."

"Seems like quite a stretch."

"We'll know soon enough. There should be certain fingerprints on that trophy, and not others. The blood residue on it will match, or it won't. Or there won't be any blood at all. I don't know. I'm trying to understand what role Martha played in all of this. Trying to understand the sequence of events."

"You said Juliet Favor didn't die from the blow to her head."

"She didn't."

"And I'm sure you don't believe Martha Lehman harmed anyone."

"I don't. That's the whole point."

With the dishes dried and put away, the Brandens took seats at the kitchen table, and their day drew to a close there, as it had begun, with pink coloring the sky. Twilight lingered, and then faded, and the neighborhood lights gave luminosity to the large snowflakes streaming down.

The front doorbell rang, and Caroline answered it and brought

163

Evelyn Carson and Cal Troyer back along the long hallway to take seats at the kitchen table. Caroline put on a pot of coffee and set out four mugs, a Texas cattle scene, a New Orleans, a Phantom of the Opera, and a San Francisco streetcar.

Evelyn Carson began directly. "Cal says Martha stopped by the church late this afternoon."

Caroline sat down across from the pastor with a hopeful expression.

Cal Troyer's long white hair was pulled back, as usual, and tied off in a ponytail. His full white beard was short and neatly trimmed. He rested his stout carpenter's arms on the tabletop and clasped his callused fingers together. There was a frown on his face.

"Sonny Favor told Martha that she might just as well go ahead and get an abortion," Cal said. "Said he'd cover all of the expenses."

"That's big of him," Caroline scoffed.

Evelyn Carson said, "I went out to Cal's church after I left, Caroline. I thought maybe she'd turn up there, sooner or later."

"Sooner, it seems," the professor said.

"She's been to some Wednesday services, from time to time," Cal said. "Today she told me that you all know she's pregnant."

"You're surprised?" Caroline asked.

"Not really," Cal said. "It's pretty easy to tell she's got a wild side. She hinted about that Friday night. I found her alone in the sanctuary about a quarter to nine."

"It's not her fault, Cal," Evelyn Carson said. "It's the old abuse she's never resolved. In cases like hers, that shows up as promiscuity."

"I wasn't just talking about sex," Cal said. "She's reckless. Seems like she doesn't too much care what happens to her."

"That's all part of the pattern, unresolved childhood issues or troubling memories and dreams," Evelyn said.

Branden thought about mentioning Martha's affair with art professor Phillips Royce, and decided against it. Instead, he said, "Cal, do you know where she went after she talked with you?"

"She made two calls from the church, and Sonny Favor came around and picked her up in his 4x4," Cal said.

"Great!" Caroline said. "That's just great."

"Did she confide in you, Cal?" Evelyn asked. "Really talk about important things?"

"Yes," Cal said simply, and stroked his beard.

The three waited.

Said Cal, "I really shouldn't tell you anything about it."

The professor rose, carried the coffeepot to the table, and poured all around.

"This decaf?" Cal asked.

Caroline nodded.

Evelyn said, "Her state of mind is fragile now, even if she is talking again. I'd rather she weren't riding around with Sonny Favor."

Branden set the carafe down, stepped to the phone, and dialed Sonny's cell phone. Into the phone he said, "Sonny? Right. Professor Branden. Is Martha with you?" With his palm cupped over the mouthpiece, he shook his head. Caroline came along beside him and leaned her ear to the receiver.

Branden next said, "We thought you'd know where she is, Sonny. I see. No, the snow is bad here, too. Then why did you let her go? For crying out loud, Sonny! Don't you think that was a bit reckless? I'd like to talk to you, Sonny. No, I've got a faculty meeting tomorrow afternoon. All right, Sunday night, then. No, your dorm lobby. You're not supposed to be inside your house, Sonny. No, I'd advise you not to do that, Sonny. Look, you just stay out of there. OK. Right. And call me if Martha comes back. OK. Yes. I'm sorry about your mother, Sonny. Yes, truly. Why would you doubt that? I hope you'll change your mind. OK, Sonny, but you're wrong. We'll leave it at that. You just make sure you're there tomorrow night. Yes, goodbye."

At the table again, the professor gave an explanation. "Sonny picked Martha up at the church. Took her back to her dorm. Outside, there was an Amish gentleman in a buggy. Martha spoke to him in Dutch dialect briefly, climbed up onto the seat, and drove off with him."

"John Schlabaugh," Caroline muttered.

"Probably," Branden said. "Sonny couldn't think of a reason to follow her. He said she was crying."

"That boy has a heart of stone," Evelyn said.

"I'm not very happy with him," Branden said. "He sounds as if he's washed his hands of her. Spoke about his new responsibilities to his family."

Caroline shook her head. "Martha doesn't need these two guys in her life, right now."

Evelyn said, "At least John Schlabaugh won't advise her to have an abortion. That could prove disastrous for her, emotionally."

Caroline nodded agreement. "Tomorrow, when we talk to John, we're going to have to get him to bring her back."

Pointedly, Cal said, "I don't think you'd better count on that."

"Why?" Branden asked.

Cal shrugged and said no more.

"Tell them about the trophy," Caroline said to her husband.

Branden gave a brief account, emphasizing the fact that the blow to the head did not kill Juliet Favor.

"Maybe all Martha did was clean off the blood and put it back on the mantel," Cal said.

"If she saw the murder, that would account for her condition this morning," Evelyn said.

Branden said, "She saw something. Probably handled the trophy, too."

"If she knows who the killer is, she's in danger," Caroline said.

"Maybe all she knows is who hit Favor on the head," Branden said. "Trouble is, that person may still think he killed Favor."

"Or she," Caroline interjected.

"Or she," Branden agreed. "That person might not know Favor was already dead."

"Would that be enough to produce the reaction we saw in Martha this morning?" Caroline asked.

"Oh, very much so," Evelyn said.

"What do you all plan to do tomorrow?" Cal asked.

Evelyn said, "I can't do anything for her, unless she comes back to see me."

"Like I said," Cal said, "I wouldn't count on that just yet."

Caroline said, "Evelyn and I have an appointment to talk with John Schlabaugh tomorrow."

"You don't sound like you care too much for him," Cal observed.

"I don't," Caroline said, eyes leveled intently at Cal.

"Hold off on that judgment, Caroline," Cal said knowingly. "John Schlabaugh is about ready to break away from his Old Order sect. I've been spending a lot of time in the scriptures with him."

"You think he might quit on the thing?" Branden asked.

"John has been in touch with Martha about this," Cal said. "He put money down on a car, and I have him counseling with the pastor at the conservative Mennonite church over south of Fredericksburg, where Martha's family goes now."

"He'd join Martha's church?" Caroline asked.

"I think so," Cal said. "It's a delicate thing at the moment. For now, Martha is with him—her choice—and he's close to a conversion breakthrough. It couldn't be a more delicate time for him, spiritually."

Caroline studied the pastor's round face and large, tranquil eyes. "We still need to talk to him," she said.

Evelyn agreed with a nod.

Cal slid his chair back and stood up. He slipped his arms into his coat and said, "I'll let you know as soon as I hear from them. In the meantime, I'm going out to her old district and nose around. There's a shoe repair shop where I know the fella likes to talk."

Out under the light of the front porch, with snow accumulating on his black felt hat, Cal asked Branden, "What does Bruce make of this whole mess?"

Branden said, "He thinks Martha is in it up to her neck."

"You remember when we caught the minister's garage on fire, trying to smoke those cigarettes?"

Branden laughed. "Bruce told his dad it was only him."

"Did you ever own up to it, Mike?"

"No."

"Neither did I," Cal said. "Too embarrassed. Bruce took a licking over that one."

"His dad wasn't the gentle type."

"No. Not at all."

Branden stuffed his hands into his coat pockets and watched snowflakes coming down, thinking about his lifelong friendships with Troyer and Robertson.

Cal said, "Mike, you're gonna want to think of Martha like you do Bruce."

Branden looked back at Cal.

"Martha is confused about her loyalties right now. She doesn't know whether she should protect someone, or whether she should tell what she knows."

"Protect whom?" Branden asked.

Cal said, "You know I can't say," and stepped off the porch into the snow.

31

AT THE home of Martha Lehman's parents in Fredericksburg, Cal Troyer accepted a cup of herb tea in the kitchen and sat with them at a round kitchen table with a red formica top. The Lehmans were dressed like ordinary English folk, though more conservatively than most. Mr. Lehman wore a plain white shirt and dark cotton slacks. He was in his evening slippers. Mrs. Lehman wore a plain pink dress with a white lace apron and white prayer cap. She produced a large manila envelope and dumped the contents, pictures of all sizes, onto the table. Mr. Lehman spread them out, and Cal saw immediately that they were all shots of one red barn, from various angles, inside and out, taken at different seasons of the year.

Mrs. Lehman said, "Martha has not been very happy with us, lately. She thinks we ruined her life, or something."

Mr. Lehman said, "She's only been home once since school started this year, and she brought all these pictures and pretty much threw them out onto the living room carpet. She kinda kicked them around with her toe, and said, 'What happened in this barn?' She was mad, really mad. Thought we could tell her something."

Mrs. Lehman said, "She thinks we have held something from her. Lord knows, Cal, we didn't know a thing. It's crazy. Why would we hurt her?"

Cal picked up one of the smaller photographs and asked, "Can I take one of these?"

Mr. Lehman said, "Sure, take as many as you like. Martha said she had photographed that old barn about a thousand times. Wanted to know why we thought she would need to go back there time and time again. She pretty much accused us of child abuse, or something. Said we let her down."

Cal asked, "You haven't seen her today?"

"No," said Mr. Lehman. "Is she all right?"

"Yes, I think so," Cal said. "But her boyfriend's mother was murdered last night, and Sheriff Robertson wants to talk to her about that."

The Lehmans looked at each other, puzzled, and Mr. Lehman said, "We haven't seen her except that one time, since she went back to school."

"I wouldn't worry too much," Cal said. "If she sees me again, I'll tell her to come out to see you."

"She won't do that," Mrs. Lehman said. "She's really mad about something."

"Then, when I have something, I'll come see you myself," Cal said.

He thanked them for the picture and left.

32

ABNER Mast had clamped a thick leather sole to a size eleven work
boot and was running a massive old stitching machine around the
edge to sew it together. Cal Troyer stood and watched. They were
in a red outbuilding behind the Mast residence about a mile west
of Charm. A fire in a potbellied stove heated the room. Overhead,
delicate silk mantles glowed at the ends of small, round gas pipes,
which crisscrossed the ceiling. Five of the mantles hissed softly with
flame, and still the room was not particularly bright.

Cal asked, "So, you knew the Lehmans?" and watched Abner's
scarred and dirty fingers work skillfully around the thick needle,
as the boot turned on the contour of its sole and the leather tight-
ened with the stitching.

"This is the hardest part," Abner said, and concentrated on the
last few inches. He finished up, cut the waxed thread with a knife,
and tossed the old boot onto the floor. In all, there were, by Cal's
count, five finished pairs on the floor, and a dozen or so left to do.
Abner's supply of new soles was sorted into cubbyholes over his
workbench. Taking up a child's boot, he chose the right size sole
and lined it up on the bottom of the boot.

Cal waited and watched.

Abner made an adjustment on his stitching machine, used an old
oilcan in places, and then glanced back at Cal. "The bishop put the
Mite on all the Lehmans when they pulled out of the congregation.
I'm not supposed to be talking about 'em."

Cal smiled. "I reckon you could tell me a few things, and it wouldn't get around."

Abner smiled too. "Can't see how it'd hurt." He worked the small boot into place on his machine and threw a few stitches before letting go. The boot was pinned by the needle. Abner walked over to the stove and pitched in another log. He was five feet, four inches tall, and his hair and beard were gray. He had the butt of a thick cigar caught in the corner of his mouth, and he used a glowing splint to light it. Some sparks caught in his beard, and he danced a bit, brushing the glowing hair out onto the floor. He pinched the cigar in his fingers and spat tobacco.

Cal laughed, and Abner said, "You think that's funny?"

Cal shrugged and said, "Bishop sees you dancing around like that, and you're gonna be out, too."

Abner laughed and put the cigar back into the corner of his mouth. He puffed on the thing several times and finished by blowing a dense cloud of blue-white smoke toward the ceiling. "Boots it was," he said. "That was the first of the Lehmans' troubles."

"How many people split off?" Cal asked.

"Well, let's see, now. There was the whole John Lehman family —thirteen, I guess. And his brothers, too. With their families, I guess maybe about fifty souls. They all went Mennonite. But it was boots as I remember the first of it."

"Had to be more than that," Cal observed.

"Oh, it was. But first John wanted his family dressed in those store-bought walking shoes. Said it'd be better for their feet."

"He was probably right," Cal said.

"I just mend them," Abner said, waving a hand at the pile of old boots on his workbench. "Truth was, John Lehman was a bible scholar, or so he thought, and he started hounding the bishop's tracks over all our little rules. Said we were all wrong to obey so many rules."

Cal said, "He's Mennonite now, so I'm guessing he preached about salvation by faith."

"That's all he talked about, Cal. Wanted to organize bible studies, teach people about faith. Said we could be certain about heaven when we die. Through faith. Saving faith, he called it. Said it was in the scriptures."

"It is," Cal said. "We are saved by grace, through faith, and not by works—the way we live our lives—so that no man can boast."

Abner shrugged. "Who's gonna keep the old ways, Cal? It matters how we live."

"I wouldn't disagree," Cal said, "but do you think that was enough to get him Mited?"

"Bishop warned him not to preach that liberal doctrine. So, yeah, they were shunned."

"Have you seen much of him since then?" Cal asked.

"You bet. He still comes around here. Drives that fancy car of his right up into my yard. I had to tell him to stop coming around. He was gonna get me shunned, too."

"I think they've got a good church now, Abner."

"I wouldn't know."

"What can you tell me about his daughter?"

"Which one? He had six."

"Martha."

"She was in the middle. Strange girl. She stopped talking one day, and he took her to a head doctor in town."

"Do you think that brought the bishop down on him harder?"

"Naw. We know about psychiatrists. We're not backward, Cal. Just like to do things the old way."

Cal nodded, tried not to smile. "You have any idea what happened to her?"

"I guess I lost track."

"She had a baby when she was fourteen. Gave it up for adoption."

Abner nodded, shrugged to indicate he had known that. "Some folks said it was John Schlabaugh's baby."

"Wasn't," Cal said.

Abner raised an eyebrow. "Nobody out here knew that."

Cal figured otherwise, but said, "Martha is in trouble again. I thought she might have been out this way."

Abner pulled his cigar out and eyed Cal closely. "She comes around to take pictures."

Cal produced the small photograph he had borrowed from the Lehmans and showed it to Mast. "You recognize this?" he asked.

Abner took the photograph in his fingers and studied it. "Sure. That was John Wengert's barn. He had the farm next to the Lehmans."

"Was?"

"It burned down a few weeks ago."

"Martha has about a hundred photographs of that barn," Cal said. "Inside and out."

"Like I say, it burned down," Abner said.

"Why do you suppose she took so many pictures of it?"

Abner Mast focused his eyes on the floorboards. "John Wengert moved up north. He's dead, now."

Cal waited, but Abner had nothing more to say.

"What happened in that barn, Abner?" Cal asked.

Mast looked into Cal's eyes, briefly, and then turned to his sewing machine. Nothing else Cal said that night convinced Abner to talk any more than he already had.

33

Sunday, November 3
Noon

CAL preached at his church for an hour and a half Sunday morning and found himself afterward at the Brandens' house for lunch. He finished a large bowl of soup and a roast beef sandwich, and took a refill of coffee when Professor Branden carried the carafe over to the table. Caroline had questioned Cal about his conversations Saturday night, and he had told of the barn photographs Martha's parents had shown him.

"I think Martha has fixated on this old barn," Cal said. "Even Abner Mast knew she'd been out several times to take the pictures. The man who had lived there when Martha was a young girl moved away about ten years ago. He's dead now. But Abner was strangely agitated to have been talking about him."

Caroline asked, "Mast is from the Lehmans' old congregation? Old Order Amish?"

"He's Beachy Amish," Cal said.

"Is there really that much of a difference?" Branden asked.

"Quite a bit, actually," Cal said. "At the simplest level, and this wouldn't at all be considered to be a thorough listing, we have the most conservative Old Order Amish, what you might call House Amish, then Beachy Amish, Church Amish, Swiss Mennonites, Old Mennonites, Wisler Mennonites, Mennonites, New Amish or Apostolic Christian, Reformed Mennonites, and most liberal, Oak Grove Mennonites up in Wayne County. They are all Anabaptist sects sprung off from the original groups led by Menno Simons and Jakob Ammann. In 1693, Ammann split off the 'Amish,' as they are now called, because he believed in the most conservative principles. Menno Simons is then the founder of the Mennonites, and they went a more liberal way. To this day, there have been dozens of splits in both branches, and it'd take a trained sociologist years to sort out the differences, and then it'd probably be wrong. Or out of date. The Lehmans split from the Mast sect over a fine point of doctrine and found a Mennonite congregation that suited them better. But other Amish groups have split over things as little as putting a side glass window in a buggy."

Caroline asked, "Is Martha a member of that Mennonite church now?"

"Not really. She has never been baptized. The Anabaptists believe in the baptism of adults only. They figure it is only an adult who can appreciate the importance and the significance of the sacrament of baptism. They believe God intends adults to accept baptism as an outward expression of their faith."

"Then was she ever a member of her old Amish church?"

"No," Cal said. "It's the same thing there. Church membership starts with baptism. That is considered to be the first act of faith. That, and a public confession of faith. Any confession of faith by an adult is immediately followed by baptism. That's what puts you into the church."

"How many congregations of Amish and Mennonite do you figure there are now?" Branden asked. "In Holmes and Wayne counties, anyway."

"Probably a hundred. Even the locals have a hard time sorting it out. And it changes every time there's a split over something like phones."

"I see a lot of Amish with cell phones now," Caroline said.

Cal shrugged. "Anything modern can cause a split."

"What do you think, then, of Martha's predicament?" Branden asked.

"She needs God in her life now, more than ever before. But she's mad at God. Mad at her parents. She's got something eating at her that she doesn't understand, and I can't see a way to help her with that. She needs someone who will understand, and stand by her through some rough times up ahead. Evelyn Carson may be the best person for that. But Martha doesn't trust authority figures right now, and she's tired of doctors. Says she just wants to be happy, but I don't think she can be, at least not under the circumstances."

34

Sunday, November 3
1:00 P.M.

THE HOUR before the Sunday faculty meeting proved to be a busy one for Branden. Phillips Royce was the first person to knock on his office door at the college.

Said Royce, "I hope you have reconsidered, Professor. About my motion, that is."

Branden got out of his chair slowly, closed the inner door to his office, and sat back down. "I'll oppose your motion, Royce," Branden said slowly, "because it is divisive and nefarious."

With forced calm, Royce responded, "You're taking this much too seriously, Mike."

Branden tapped his fingers on the desk and thought carefully about his next statement. Eventually, he said, "I know about you and Martha Lehman."

"Just what is it that you think you know?"

"I know that you two had an affair, Phillips."

Royce fumbled for his pipe, and Branden said, "Please do not smoke in my office."

Royce slipped the pipe back into the pocket of his sport coat. Then he fiddled with the long, pointed ends of his waxed mustache. Flustered, he said, "What are you going to do about it?"

"I intend to speak against your motion this afternoon."

"Nothing more?"

"Of course more, Phillips. Much more, eventually, if you force my hand. But nothing at this juncture."

"This is hardly the age, Mike, to go Puritan on the issue. She's twenty-three years old, for God's sake."

"She is your student, Phillips."

"It only happened once."

"That hardly matters to me."

"I'll deny it."

"I'm not pressing the issue," Branden said. "I only had that information second-hand, to begin with."

"Martha didn't tell you?"

"Martha isn't talking to me right now."

"She may be Mennonite, Mike, but she's a wildcat."

"You're disgracing yourself, now, Phillips," Branden said. "There is no reason extant for a professor, in a position of power and authority, to have intimate relations with a student."

"What's she saying? That it wasn't consensual?"

"Martha hasn't told me anything. By your own words, you've as much as admitted it."

"So, Professor, I ask again. What do you intend to do?"

"If Martha comes through this episode safely, I'll do nothing more than file a private complaint with the president. He'll have to decide whether or not he wants to take it to the board of trustees for action."

"What do you mean 'episode'?" Royce asked.

"Martha Lehman is pregnant."

Royce's face turned pale. Branden watched him carefully and decided that Royce had not known.

Royce looked away and then back again. "It can't be mine," he said, with relief showing on his face. "That was last January."

"Don't you think your affair with her will have had some negative emotional impact on her ability to finish your tutorial?"

"Yes, well, I suppose."

"Then I suggest, Phillips, that you do whatever it takes to see that she succeeds in that tutorial. Help her any way you can, so long as it doesn't besmirch her integrity."

"I don't see that it is any of your business to tell me how to run a tutorial, Professor."

"And I don't see that I'd have any choice but to ruin you, Professor, if your sorry conduct has caused Ms. Lehman lasting harm."

"I'll work something out. Where is she?"

"For the moment, I do not know."

"Then what do you expect me to do?"

"Work it through, Phillips. I'm not your babysitter."

"Really, Mike, you've gone too far."

"If anything, I haven't gone far enough. Now, get out of my office. I have a debate to prepare for."

"You can't just leave it hanging like this."

"I can, and I will," Branden said, heat flooding his cheeks and neck. He stood up behind his desk. "You'll either make it right with Martha Lehman or I'll have you up on charges in a grievance procedure."

Royce stood and took Branden's measure with a long, fierce look into his eyes. Then he turned briskly and left.

AS ROYCE left, Branden's email delivered a message, which he scanned quickly:

> Mike. No fingerprints other than Henry DiSalvo's on the
> trophy. Blood trace on the trophy matches Favor's type. Take
> a week or so to have a full DNA match. Can you get a water
> sample from Dick Pomeroy's lab?
> Missy.

CHEMISTRY professor Dick Pomeroy came next into the spacious office and stood by the corner windows. "You've always had the best view, Mike," he said, and then took a seat in front of Branden's desk.

"You want some coffee, Dick? Something to drink?"

"Naw. I'm just curious. Won't take a minute. Heard you'll be arguing against Royce's motion."

"I will," Branden said.

"Just wanted to check," Pomeroy said. "Can always use the help from your side of the street."

"I figure he's attacking the fundamental assumptions on which this college was built," Branden said. "And I never thought we were on opposite sides of the street—history and chemistry."

"Too true, Mike. Too true. Well, that's all," Pomeroy said, and rose.

"Before you go," Branden said, "I'd like you to consider giving Sonny Favor an extension on Monday's exam."

"Very reasonable, under the circumstances."

"Thank you. Another thing," Branden said, holding to his seat.

"Name it."

"Melissa Taggert could use a sample of the water from your lab."

"No problem, Mike."

"Is it OK, then, if I stop by after faculty meeting?"

"No problem at all," Pomeroy said, and left.

PRESIDENT Arne Laughton appeared in the professor's office only fifteen minutes before the start of the faculty meeting.

After pleasantries, Branden said, "I understand a little of Juliet Favor's estate goes to the college, Arne."

The president said, "Where did you hear that, Mike?"

"It's going to cause squabbles over program funding, Arne. How are you going to handle that?"

"We don't have the money yet," Laughton said, "but the board will make those decisions."

"That's why I wanted to talk to you. You've got a chance to show some leadership here, Arne. The kind of leadership that will set your name in stone for a hundred years. Organize a joint faculty-board committee to plan how this money will be used."

"The board usually holds such decisions to itself, Mike. You know that."

"Yes, but if you sold that idea hard, the board would go along with it."

"Have you forgotten that I serve as president only at the pleasure of the board?"

"Show some backbone on this one, Arne."

"This is hardly the time to haggle over money. Juliet Favor isn't even in the ground yet, Mike."

"Let's think toward the future, Arne. Let's get past this idiotic debate Royce is precipitating, and organize some real faculty input, for a change, into how Favor's money will be used."

"You know the board handles the big money issues."

"Right, Arne. I am suggesting you put your stamp on this institution by elevating academic concerns back into prominence."

WALT Camry, English professor, trudged with Branden through the snow to the faculty meeting in Bartlett Hall, adjacent to the new chemistry building. "Mike, I hope you'll argue for the humanities," he said.

"I plan to argue in favor of the true liberal arts agenda. That includes sciences and the humanities."

"You're not going to make many friends today, Mike."

"On the contrary. I hope to convert a lot of people. Remind them how things used to be."

"Technology has advanced to the point where there is a divide between science and humanities, Mike. Anybody can see that."

"None of our students needs to be afraid of the sciences, Walt."

"Well, they are. You know that as well as anyone."

"Phillips Royce's motion, if passed, will divide the college. Just debating the thing has already done too much of that."

"I'm sorry you feel that way, Mike."

"Are you afraid I might persuade you, Walt?"

"Not likely, Professor."

"But you will listen."

"Of course. That's what we're all about, here. Keeping an open mind."

35

CAROLINE drove her small truck down off the icy road to Charm, Ohio, onto the vast, unplowed tourist parking lot of the Bavarian cheese factory, and slid to a stop in the deep snow at the very edge of the culvert at the front of the lot. Evelyn got out on the passenger's side and examined the snow-covered ditch, the wheels of the truck on the driver's side perched to slip over the edge. The psychiatrist motioned Caroline forward with a tentative wave, but as Caroline let out the clutch, the back left tire slipped off the pavement, and the rear of the truck dropped three feet into the ditch. After trying unsuccessfully to extricate the truck, Caroline climbed out on the passenger's side and stood in two feet of unplowed snow to call AAA for a tow. If she hadn't been so worried about Martha Lehman, she might almost have considered it funny. She finished her call, closed up the phone, and scanned the quiet country scene in white. Across a field at the far end of the parking lot came a one-horse sleigh.

The sleigh glided smoothly forward in the deep snow, horse snorting giant puffs of white steam from its flaring nostrils. John Schlabaugh climbed down from the seat.

Evelyn Carson asked, "Is Martha at your place, John?"

"At the house," he said, "in town. I live in town, now."

"We need to see her," Caroline said.

"I think you need to come," Schlabaugh said. "She has nightmares, and they were bad last night. Early this morning she took some of Sonny Favor's pills. Now I can't wake her up."

36

CAROLINE would likely never forget the heartache of that frantic Sunday afternoon sleigh ride to John Schlabaugh's house on the edge of the sleepy burg of Charm. Racing across the snow-covered stubble of a cornfield. Splashing through the ford on the little stream south of the cheese factory. Cresting the hill and then coming into town over snow-covered lawns. The runners of the sleigh clenching the bare pavement and throwing sparks as they crossed a road. The relentless lash of the whip.

Then calling the rescue squad on her cell phone. Riding in the ambulance with Martha, and waiting alone in the emergency room at Joel Pomerene Hospital for doctors to attend to Martha and for Evelyn and John to arrive in Schlabaugh's new car. Carson went in to help with Martha, leaving Caroline seated next to Schlabaugh in the busy hallway. Neither talked until Evelyn came out briefly to report that Martha had taken only a few pills. Desryl. A first-generation antidepressant, with a strong sedative effect. The pregnancy might have been compromised.

As the news sank in, Caroline turned her attention slowly to John. To him she said, "This is too much like before, Mr. Schlabaugh. You in the waiting room and Martha in the emergency room. You'll forgive me if I don't sing your praises."

"This is not something I have chosen," he said softly. "Neither was it then."

"You almost killed her," Caroline charged.

"I loved her. Still do, Mrs. Branden."

"You've got a funny way of showing it."

Schlabaugh sighed. He rubbed the shiny denim on his knees and tossed his black, broad-brimmed hat on the seat beside him. He struggled out of a worn denim jacket, turned to face Caroline, and asked, "Will you listen to my side of this?"

Caroline stared at him, thought, softened, cast her eyes to the floor, sighed, and said, "OK, why not?"

"I don't know where to start," Schlabaugh said and unhooked his denim vest. He combed his fingers back through long black hair, and shook his head. "Do you know any of the details of what happened to Martha when she was young?"

Caroline said, "Her psychiatrist hasn't told us much about that," and waited.

Schlabaugh seemed to gather his memories for a difficult task, and then began. "Martha stopped talking when she was six. It was spring, and one day she just stopped. Nothing persuaded her to talk again, at least for many years. After her son was born—she was fourteen then—it was Dr. Carson who finally pulled her through, I guess.

"We eventually got used to it, us kids in the district. Martha didn't talk. It was like saying she had brown hair. That was Martha. It didn't seem like too much was wrong with her. She just wouldn't talk, you see. But, there was a problem. A bad man in the congregation who never married. Name was John Wengert. I partly figured it out the year Martha was pregnant, by the way she acted around him. At the Sunday meetings and such. Other girls were involved, I think.

"That man was a bad one, you'd better believe it. I confronted him. He moved to Wisconsin before Martha's son was born. Then, a couple of years ago, we heard he had accidentally strangled himself with a rope attached to a beam in his barn. Had his pants down when they found him. Somebody called him a 'gasper,' whatever that is.

"Anyways, Martha seemed OK after he moved away. Well, at

least she started talking again. She seemed better. But her family had trouble with other folks in the district because of her, and they converted to conservative Mennonite. The Bishop told us we weren't allowed to talk to them anymore, after that. She finished high school with a G.E.D., but I guess you'll know more about that than I do.

"But the thing is, lately, I've had my doubts about Amish ways, too. Cal Troyer helped them convert, so I've been studying with him, like her parents did. Now my own family won't talk to me because I've bought a car, so I guess I might as well go ahead and finish the thing. Join Martha's church. That was my idea, anyways, but it seems, now, that Martha has fallen away. Backslidden. She's not interested in church like she used to be.

"Cal Troyer says I should give her time. Says if she was molested as a child that she might need to work through a lot of mental problems before she gets well. So, I have waited, and it's been hard, you see, to watch her take up with the likes of Sonny Favor. It's like she's looking for trouble. But I just hold on and wait. Hope she notices I'm not backward Amish anymore.

"But it's been hard. I wanted to take care of her when her son was born. Didn't matter to me whose kid it was. I told her I'd marry her. I think by then she knew she couldn't stay Amish. Maybe I stand a better chance, now.

"Mostly, now, I'm waiting. Yep—biding my time. I don't have a farm, you see. I got a job as an electrician for a contractor out near Apple Creek. My old man used to wire up camper trailers for a living, so I learned the trade. I've sure gone English, you'd better believe it. House in the city. Car. Job off the farm. Maybe she'll see I can take care of her, now. I'd want her to finish college, too. Use her photography. That's an art, you know. Amish don't have much time for art, and they don't tolerate photography at all.

"But Martha is going to have to get rid of her nightmares. They're bad. I mean really bad. Last night, she just about cried all night long. And that Favor boy has been giving her pills. Silly weed, too. You know, marijuana. Drugs for a pregnant woman, for crying out loud. She says her nightmares seem so real—she's back as a young girl, and that man on top of her. I don't think she realizes, yet, what that means. Or maybe she does, and that's what's driving her into the nut house. I don't think she's slept in months.

"But I wish she knew I am not going to be Amish anymore. Maybe Dr. Carson can explain that to her. I tried last night, but I think she was too loony to hear. Amish don't have a sure hope of salvation, you know. No sure hope of heaven. That's the problem. Cal Troyer can explain it good enough. All their salvation is based on living right—following all the rules. Endless rules, and then you can't even be sure of heaven.

"But the Mennonites understand Faith and Grace. It's all in Ephesians and Galatians. I don't think Amish read these epistles too carefully. They think the only way to heaven is to live a good life. Not a bad idea, I suppose, but it doesn't leave any room for faith. We are saved by grace through faith—'not by works, so that no man can boast.' I'm hoping Martha still remembers that. I have a feeling she's going to need it.

"Last night scared me, you'd better believe it. She acted like she was a little girl all over again. All of a sudden, she wouldn't talk again. I remembered how she was, when we were kids. Back then, she just didn't talk, and that was all. Now, she is also very frightened. She doesn't believe she can ever be safe again.

"Now, it's like the old hurting from childhood can hurt her again, only this time it's worse. This time, it's out in the open for her to see. I want to help her. Make her safe. Marry her, Mrs. Branden. I hope you can accept that. Hope you understand. If Martha is in trouble again, it won't be the likes of Sonny Favor who will help her. He won't even try. No, Mrs. Branden. I'm the one for her. I've changed my life for her. Sonny Favor is damaged goods. It's too late for him. He'll be brought low by a love of money, just like his mother.

"You blame me because I took Martha to a midwife. You blame me because she almost died. But I got her here in time, didn't I? I've been the one for Martha all along, Mrs. Branden. You'd better believe it."

37

Sunday, November 3
4:45 P.M.

DICK Pomeroy turned the key to unlock his lab in the chemistry building and said, "You carried the day at faculty meeting, Mike. Fabulous speech."

Branden followed the chemist into the lab and said, "I guess it wasn't such an unpopular position, after all."

"Thought Royce was going to pop a vessel!" Pomeroy said and laughed. "You had all the scientists to start with. But you swung the others, too. Well done, Professor."

"You put your two cents in," Branden said.

"Pesticide hydrolysis," Pomeroy said with a self-congratulatory tone. "Couldn't let them drone on about the environment without acquainting them with the facts!"

"A lot of people don't like science, Dick. You have to allow for that."

"Doesn't mean I have to let them off the hook when they get the facts wrong. Pesticides aren't 'an eternal scourge.'"

"You nearly lost even me with that one," Branden said.

"President cut me off. Point is, modern pesticides can be made to hydrolyze in time. That makes them less dangerous. Rain and ground water eventually chew 'em up. If our students took enough science, they'd know that."

"We haven't all heard the term hydrolysis before," Branden said.

"Reaction with water. All it means, Mike. Lots of things hydro-lyze. Pesticides, for one, if they're built right."

Pomeroy put on his lab coat and stood at one of the black bench-tops in his lab. He used a small brush to sweep powder from the top of one of his electronic balances. "See this?" he said. "I have to start over every year with new kids. Students can't even bother to clean up after themselves."

Branden studied the room. "Your labs seem immaculate, Dick," he countered.

Pomeroy sighed. "I try," he said. At one of the sinks, he began rinsing beakers and hanging them upside down on pegs to dry. "Anyway," he said, "thanks for the help today."

Branden said, "No problem. But, as I said, your comments helped, too."

"I just think that if the Greens are going to express an opinion, they ought to know some science, first. They have to take those science classes to be liberally educated."

"I couldn't agree more," Branden said.

On a shelf, there were several dozen bound notebooks, each labeled on the spine, some in English and some in Japanese. "Are these your lab books?" Branden asked.

"Right," Pomeroy said, and dried his hands on his lab coat. He took one down and opened it to a random page. "I send samples out to various companies for bio-assays. Looking for new drugs."

"You get the samples in Peru?" Branden asked.

"Right. Forests and mountains. We bring the samples back, isolate the compounds here, and then I have patent arrangements with the companies."

"Lucrative?" Branden asked.

"Let's just say I haven't had to write any government grant proposals in recent years."

"Good for the students, I'll bet," Branden said.

"I hire quite a few, yes. Chemistry majors, mostly," Pomeroy said, and replaced the lab book, aligning the spine carefully with the others on the shelf.

"I suppose you get Favor money, too," Branden said.

"Yes, a good amount," Pomeroy said.

Branden remembered the rumor about the Pomeroy and Favor affair, couldn't remember where he had heard it first, and decided to let that drop.

Pomeroy said, "Now that there's to be extra money for the college, perhaps Favor money could get in the research game even more."

"It looks as if there'll be plenty of money for everyone," Branden said. "More money all around. That's the fair way."

"If it's spent the right way," Pomeroy observed, and swabbed out the spigot on a water purifier.

"I'm pushing Arne for faculty input on a committee to handle the new money," Branden said.

"Fat chance, Mike."

"I've got to try."

"The board of trustees has probably already spent that money on buildings."

"I'd rather see it spent on academic programs," Branden said. "Not that buildings aren't important."

Pomeroy put glassware away in a drawer and turned in place to inspect the lab. Satisfied, he took off his lab coat and sat down at a small desk in the corner. He motioned Branden to a seat on a lab stool. Then, he snapped his fingers and said, "You wanted a water sample." At the water purifier, he said, "My water purifying unit has been on the fritz for a while."

"That's OK," Branden said. "Whatever water you've been using. For some tests Coroner Taggert is running."

Pomeroy dispensed a sample into a little bottle with a ground glass stopper and handed it to Branden.

Branden said, "Is this the same type of bottle you gave to Juliet Favor?"

"Yep. DMSO."

"DMSO and water," Branden said. "Why the water?"

Pomeroy said, "To dilute it. Straight DMSO used to make her

nauseous. I don't know what's wrong with this purifier, though. It's been a little out of whack for a couple of weeks."

Branden held up the bottle and eyed the clear liquid. "I understand Sally Favor worked for you, once," he said.

"One summer and the following fall semester. I needed someone who could work up the bio samples, and she was in the molecular biology program. She was good at chemistry, too. Sonny, I am afraid, is another story."

"I'm grateful for the extension on his exam," Branden said, with his hand on the doorknob.

"Sure," Pomeroy said. "Think nothing of it."

38

Sunday, November 3
5:00 P.M.

ONCE Martha had been transferred from the emergency room to a room on the second floor of the hospital, Evelyn Carson came out to the small waiting area at the end of the hall and sat next to Caroline, on a couch facing John Schlabaugh.

"How is she?" Caroline asked.

"Can I see her?" Schlabaugh asked.

"Better, and no," Evelyn replied to the two questions.

Schlabaugh, dejected, slouched back in his seat.

Caroline asked, "What can you tell us?"

"I can't discuss everything," Evelyn said, "but she's out of the woods, as they say. It was an accidental overdose, as I told you before."

"What can I do to help?" Caroline asked, ignoring Schlabaugh.

Evelyn motioned to John and said, "Mr. Schlabaugh may eventually be in a better position to help than anyone."

"You said I couldn't see her," Schlabaugh said, still slouched.

"Not at the moment," Evelyn said. "But, I would like you to be available in the next couple of weeks. She'll need your help to remember and to understand many bad things that I think happened to her as a child. You may be the key to her being able to face her nightmares. Are you up to that, Mr. Schlabaugh?"

Said John, nodding, "I'd do anything for Martha."

"What's to be done right now?" Caroline asked.

"There are several issues, now," Evelyn said. "First, Martha is confused about Sonny Favor. That relationship appears to be over. Sonny offered her $20,000 last night to have an abortion."

Caroline groaned and shook her head. Schlabaugh slapped his knee hard, and his cheeks flushed crimson.

"I don't think she is considering it," Evelyn said. "An abortion would be unfortunate. There are too many issues to deal with, now. Sonny Favor must be a brat."

"What about college?" Caroline asked.

Evelyn said, "Martha has to face her problems, now, Caroline. School will have to take a back seat to therapy."

Caroline began to cry softly, tears spilling freely onto her cheeks.

Evelyn took Caroline's hand. "Martha's nightmares," she said, "are most probably real memories coming forward from the subconscious. Memories she suppressed as a child. She won't be ready for school for a very long time. She is beginning to realize that her memories are not just bad dreams. She's just starting to realize that the nightmares aren't going to go away just yet. There's a lot of confusion, too. It'll take time to sort the real memories from imagined ones. For the moment, she talks in a child's soft whisper when she describes some of them. There must have been a bad neighbor."

Schlabaugh said, "Yes, he's dead, now."

"That may be most unfortunate," Evelyn said.

"Why?" Caroline said. "I say good riddance."

"It prevents her from confronting her abuser," Evelyn said. "That sometimes makes the healing harder, because there isn't a simple route to closure, when your tormentor is dead."

39

Sunday, November 3
5:15 P.M.

PROFESSOR Branden carried the water sample into Joel Pomerene Hospital late that Sunday afternoon, expecting to leave it at the desk out front for Missy Taggert. Instead, the lab was open. He found Missy working, and delivered the vial personally.

"Working late on a Sunday?" he asked. "Favor was only murdered Friday."

Missy took the vial of water and said, "Trying to get ahead on this one, Mike. Bruce and I have concert tickets in Chicago. We'll be leaving this evening."

Branden smiled. "That's the water from Dick Pomeroy's lab," he said and pointed at the bottle.

"Is it tap water or RO from his scrubber?" Missy asked.

"RO?"

"Reverse Osmosis," Missy explained. "Dick has a water purifier. A purple and white contraption with a spigot on the end of a flexible hose."

"Then that's RO water," Branden said. "It ought to be the purest."

Missy drew a sample into a small syringe. At one of her instruments, she injected the sample and watched the computer screen next to the machine. Once the trace was complete, she displayed the graph, overlaid one from computer memory, and found them to align almost perfectly. "Some peaks are shorter or taller," she said, "but that's considered a perfect match."

"What are you matching?" Branden asked.

"This new water sample and the water that was mixed in with the DMSO bottle I found out at Favor's place."

"They match that well?" Branden asked.

"Enough to say that Pomeroy got his water from the same spigot. Somebody ought to tell him his RO system is marginal, though."

"He said that himself," Branden said.

"It's just a matter of switching in two new scrubber cartridges," Missy said, and placed the medicine bottle on a shelf.

"I can tell you more about how Favor died," Missy said. "Good old-fashioned heart attack."

"You're kidding," Branden said.

"Her heart stopped. That's all. Whoever clobbered her over the head, they were wasting their time. Favor was dead long before that."

"Not much blood from the head wound, then," Branden surmised. "Her heart had stopped pumping."

"Right."

Branden thought about Martha Lehman. He said, "You found Favor's blood on the rugby trophy?"

"And on Martha Lehman's apron," Missy said, motioning to the benchtop where she had laid the apron down for analysis.

"You think the heart attack was natural causes, then?"

"I have no reason to suspect otherwise."

"No fingerprints on the rugby trophy, other than Henry DiSalvo's?"

"Right. Bruce has a theory."

Branden crossed his arms and leaned back against the lab bench.

Missy said, "The theory is that Martha Lehman took the heavy trophy upstairs, hit Favor over the head, carried the trophy back downstairs, dropped it on the marble floor—and there's your star crack in the marble—wiped off blood and all the fingerprints, and set it up on the shelf backwards, because she didn't know which was the front and which was the back. Then, Henry DiSalvo noticed it, and turned it around."

Branden tapped his foot nervously and thought. "Trouble is," he said shortly, "I can't picture Martha Lehman trying to hurt anyone."

"Bruce sure can," Missy said. "He's on his way upstairs to question her now."

"Upstairs?" Branden pressed.

"They brought her in with an apparent overdose, Mike. She's had some kind of nervous breakdown. Caroline and Evelyn brought her in, and Bruce just went up before you got here."

Branden ran out of the lab and took the stairs two at a time.

40

Sunday, November 3
5:25 P.M.

ABRUPTLY, Sheriff Robertson pushed through the stairwell door
on the second floor of Pomerene Hospital, with two deputies in tow.
He marched up to Evelyn Carson and said, "You've got Martha
Lehman here."

The two deputies continued down the hall, and took positions
outside Martha's room. Evelyn Carson bounded to her feet and
said, "I can't let you see her. She's too fragile now."

"I'm gonna see her, Evelyn," Bruce said. "Right now. It's Juliet
Favor's blood on her apron, and I have plenty of questions for that
girl, let me tell you."

Dr. Carson buttonholed a nurse on the floor, marched to
Martha's room, and positioned herself and the nurse in front of
the door. Robertson came forward slowly, tucking his shirttail into
his pants. He was still breathing hard from the climb up the stairs.
He brushed a handkerchief across his sweaty forehead and said,
"You're gonna have to step aside, Evelyn."

Carson said, "She's my patient, Bruce, and I'm telling you, right
now, that she is in critical condition. You're staying out, and that's
final."

"We're going in," Robertson announced, and took a step toward the door.

Dr. Carson and the nurse blocked his way. Carson said, "There's
no need to traumatize her, Bruce. This girl is emotionally and mentally crippled, and you'll only make it worse."

"She's to be questioned at the very least, and perhaps even arrested," Robertson said, and one of the deputies took out a pair of handcuffs.

"I'll get an injunction," Carson said.

"Do that," Robertson said.

"It'll go badly for you, Bruce," Evelyn reasoned, "if I advise against this as her physician, and your actions harm my patient." She read a softening in the sheriff's expression and added, "I promise you, she's not going anywhere. There's no need to arrest her, and I'd rather you didn't even question her at this time."

Robertson relaxed and took a step back.

To Deputy Armbruster he said, "Stan, you're posted on this door. If anyone brings Ms. Lehman out, you're to inform me." To Evelyn Carson, he added, "And I'm telling you, Evelyn, right now, that Martha Lehman is a material witness in the attempted murder of Juliet Favor. That means I can put her in jail if I think she's gonna bolt."

At that point, Professor Branden came through the stairwell door at the end of the hall. He appraised the crowd in front of Martha's door, and marched up to Robertson. As he approached, he saw one of the deputies putting handcuffs back in the pouch on his duty belt. To Robertson, he snapped, "I know what you're doing, Bruce, and you're wrong!"

Robertson drew the professor aside and spoke quietly, but forcefully. "At the very least, Mike, she's a material witness, or an accomplice. I think she tried to murder Juliet Favor. The blood on her apron, and on the trophy, both match Juliet Favor's. So does the blood in Sonny Favor's Lexus, which Daniel Bliss saw parked at the Favor mansion just before dawn. The last known driver was Martha Lehman."

"And you know full well," Branden said, heated, "that Favor was dead long before anyone cracked her skull."

"Before Martha Lehman cracked her skull," Robertson countered.

Impulsively, Branden said, "For all we know, Sonny Favor cracked her skull." The thought startled him as he said it. Somehow, giving voice to the idea brought it to the fore in his mind, and he scrambled mentally to align puzzle pieces. Yes, that all fits, he thought. "Probably, Bruce," he said, "Martha saw Sonny, or someone, with that trophy and did nothing more than clean up someone else's mess." Privately, Branden was thinking rapidly about Sonny Favor. Where had he been? What had he done? Slept all night in his room? Probably not. So strong was the professor's conviction that Martha had not harmed Juliet Favor, whether dead or alive at the time, that he realized, finally, that he should long ago have considered the reasons why Martha might have carried the trophy downstairs and wiped off the blood. It was Sonny, he realized. She had been protecting Sonny. Check that, he thought, to be sure. Robertson would not accept pure conjecture. "Bruce," he said, "you may be right. Martha Lehman is a witness. But nothing more than that."

"You're guessing, now, Professor," Robertson said.

"I know. I can't bring myself to believe that Martha would have struck Juliet Favor with anything, much less a weapon like that heavy trophy."

"You've got a blind spot about Martha Lehman," Robertson said, and studied the professor's expression.

Branden turned, walked slowly back to the waiting room near the stairs, and sat in a low armchair. He saw the morgue in his mind. Martha Lehman's bloody apron, with blood wiped up after the blow to Favor's head. A new vision of Sonny Favor. Attempted murder? Not by Martha. He was sure of that. The heart attack? Implausible. And the timeline? Complicated in the extreme. His mind wandered the possibilities. There was so very much more to do. Talk to Sonny Favor, tonight. Bliss too, a key witness, and he probably doesn't even know it. And Sally Favor, as soon as possible. All the evidence to sort through, again. Because nothing seemed right, at all. Because Juliet Favor, as fit as she evidently was, was an unlikely candidate for a heart attack. Somehow, Branden thought, all of the pieces of this puzzle were going to fit.

41

Sunday, November 3
7:15 P.M.

BRANDEN arrived early Sunday night in the lobby of Sonny Favor's dorm and waited in the first-floor sitting room, in a high-backed, upholstered chair near the fireplace. The time for their appointment came and went. Branden called up to Sonny's room twice and then decided to leave. As he headed for the door, he heard from behind Sally Favor's voice, and turned to see her standing in the lobby with Jenny Radcliffe.

"Sonny's not coming, Professor Branden," Sally said. "I'm sorry. I know he was supposed to meet you here, but he's just not coming."

Branden asked the women to join him in the sitting room by the fire. They took seats there, the girls on a sofa and Branden in the high-backed chair, and Branden said, "You don't sound too happy about this, Sally."

"He's such a screw-up, Dr. Branden. I don't think he's ever going to be OK."

"Where is he?" Branden asked.

Sally shrugged. "We don't exactly know. He drove to Wooster and took the family jet back to New York City. That was early this afternoon."

"Have you talked much with him, Sally?" Branden asked. "I'm worried about his state of mind now. I don't think he slept all through Friday night, like he said he did."

"He didn't," Sally said pointedly. "He's a wreck, Dr. Branden."

"And a vicious little monster," Jenny added.

Sally sighed and smiled bravely. "He told me he's in charge now. Said I had my own money and there wasn't anything he could do to stop that. As far as he was concerned, he was all that was left of the family, and I shouldn't bother trying to get in touch with him anymore."

"So, you're out," Branden said. "But I understand you have plenty of your own money now."

"Money isn't everything, Doc," Sally said and smiled weakly. "Sonny is the only family I've got now, and he is never going to be OK. He'll be an emotional cripple all of his life, because of our mother."

"I think he might have tried to kill your mother, Sally," Branden said.

Sally nodded and began to cry. Jenny put her arms around her and drew her close. Branden offered her a handkerchief.

Sally blew her nose and said, "I seem to be making a collection of men's handkerchiefs this weekend."

Branden looked to Jenny, who said, "Sergeant Niell gave her one of his, yesterday morning."

Branden nodded. "Did Sonny tell you anything about what he did Friday night?" he asked.

Sally said, "Yes, Professor. He managed to say quite a lot, but in dribbles. Muttered a lot. He's messed up. We took rooms at Hotel Millersburg, and he paced around like a caged animal. Kept calling himself The Eunuch."

"Where did he come up with that?" Branden asked.

"I used to call him that," Sally said. She blew her nose again and resumed her account. "It took us several hours to piece the whole story together. We thought he was exhausted. Maybe unbalanced from all the drinking he'd been doing. We finally got to sleep early Sunday morning, and Jenny and I slept in. Then, by this afternoon, we realized he was gone. We barely managed to get him on his cell phone up at the airport outside of Wooster."

"It sounds as if you know something, Sally," Branden said.

"Sonny used to hate it when I called him The Eunuch. Now he's calling himself that."

Branden said gently, "It'll help if you tell me what you know, Sally. It'll help you, and it may help Sonny."

Sally sat up stiffly and said, "Sonny hit her over the head with something." She started crying again, softly.

Jenny said, "At least that is what we believe, Professor. Sonny hasn't been too coherent. He complained that 'somebody beat him to her.' Kinda like he couldn't even do that one thing right by himself."

"That fits with what I've been thinking," Branden said. "It's complicated, but I don't believe Sonny killed your mother."

"He tried to," Sally said, calmer now.

"Probably," Branden said. "But Martha Lehman seems to have cleaned up after him, and now she's in trouble with the sheriff. It would help if you could remember precisely what he said."

Jenny looked at Sally. Sally shrugged. Jenny said, "He said, 'Finally got the nerve to do it, and she was already dead, sprawled face down on the end of the bed.' He must have gone ahead and hit her anyway, just out of frustration."

Branden thought for several minutes and then asked, "Can you come down to the jail to make an official statement about this?"

Sally said, "I don't think I should get him into trouble like that."

"He's already in trouble, Sally," Branden said. "You'd be saving him from a more serious charge. You'd be able to clear up the fact that Sonny found her dead before he hit her. You'd also be saving Martha Lehman a whole lot of trouble, since she does think Sonny killed your mother, and she tried to clean up after him. I think she's the one who put your mother under the covers, wiped up what little blood there was, and took the trophy back downstairs. She couldn't have known which way was the front, so she put the trophy up backwards, and then Mr. DiSalvo saw the mistake."

"OK," Sally said, tentatively. "If you think so."

"I do," Branden said.

"Now?" Sally asked.

"Soon," Branden said. "But there's something else you can help me with. I need to know all about your work with Professor Pomeroy."

"The science, travel, what part?"

"Everything," Branden said. "Everything you did in Peru, all the follow-up, back in the lab. What he did and what you did for him. Everything."

"That could take some time," Sally said.

"It's important."

"OK," Sally said. "I didn't think I'd get the job when I applied for it, because I'm not a chemistry major. But he said he'd found something down there that required the work of a molecular biologist."

"That's precisely what I'm interested in," Branden said.

"It's complicated," Sally said.

"I have time," Branden said. "I'll make time."

42

Sunday, November 3
9:30 P.M.

BRANDEN listened to Sally Favor for more than an hour, asking detailed questions at times and listening intently at others. Having heard what he needed, he drove downtown to Hotel Millersburg and found the room where Daniel Bliss was staying. When he knocked on the door, Daniel answered and admitted the professor in silence. Branden took off his coat and draped it over the back of an armchair, in which he took a seat. He sat in a larger chair on the other side of a small, round table. Bliss waited for Branden to speak.

Branden began by saying, "I know Sonny has flown back to New York."

Bliss nodded noncommittally.

"I also know he did not kill his mother," Branden said.

Bliss remained quiet.

Next, Branden summarized the physical evidence and his theory of what Martha Lehman had done with the rugby trophy. Bliss listened without reaction.

Last, Branden said, "Finally, Mr. Bliss, I'd be grateful if you would tell me about Ms. Favor's medicine bottles."

Bliss looked back at Branden stolidly and eventually said, "If what you say is true, Mr. Favor cannot be charged."

Branden replied, "Perhaps only with molestation of a corpse."

"Do you think Sheriff Robertson still intends to search my house?"

"If I'm right, Mr. Bliss, that won't be necessary."

"And Miss Sally?"

"She's in the clear, again, if I am right."

"And how do you plan to prove that you are right?"

Branden told him.

Bliss nodded and said, "Three bottles, Professor. I put two empty bottles in the wastebasket in Ms. Favor's bathroom. She had cast them to the floor in her bedroom. The third bottle was the one I found for her in her bedroom. It was on the dresser. Once she had used some of it downstairs, I carried it back up and put it on her nightstand, where she would be sure to find it. Then I put her medicine cabinet back together, so she could find her brush. She brushes her hair every night before retiring. I put the brush and comb on the bottom shelf, and the perfumes on the second shelf, just the way she likes it, with general medicines on the upper two shelves. Then I came downstairs for the last time."

43

Sunday, November 3
11:20 P.M.

BACK on the college heights on the east side of Millersburg, Branden rang the doorbell at the president's mansion. He spoke with Arne Laughton for several minutes and took possession of a campus master key from the reluctant president. In the chemistry building on the other side of campus, Branden keyed himself into Dick Pomeroy's lab and switched on the lights. He stepped to the shelves where Pomeroy kept his lab books, and took down the one corresponding to the year that Sally Favor had worked for the chemist. He paged through the book, plus several that followed, and finished by reading the entries in several books whose spines bore the names of pharmaceutical companies.

At midnight, he phoned Henry DiSalvo at home, and waited until the disgruntled lawyer had finished sputtering his objections to being awakened at that hour. As with Bliss, Branden explained his theory of Juliet Favor's murder, leaving out the scientific details, and concluded by saying, "So I think you can see why I'd be interested in Yabusan Pharmaceuticals."

DiSalvo said, "Well, you're right, Mike. It was to be sold. Juliet had slated a good dozen companies to be sold in the next few months. It was part of her simplification scheme, so Sonny could take over the business someday."

"But would Pomeroy have known?" Branden asked.

"Well, yes," DiSalvo said. "He's on the board of directors."

44

Monday, November 4
8:10 A.M.

BEFORE his ten o'clock Civil War class Monday morning, Professor Branden let himself back into Dick Pomeroy's lab. At the water purifier, he ran out about a liter of water from the spigot, and dispensed the last few milliliters into a small, clean test tube he found on the rack over the sink. He put a cork in the test tube, slipped it into his shirt pocket, and sat down to wait for the chemist. As Pomeroy came through the door, Branden stood up and held out the test tube, saying, "This one is a fresh sample, Dick. Care to guess what Melissa Taggert is going to find when I have her test it?"

Calmly, Pomeroy hung his coat on a hook and set his briefcase on his desk. He crossed to the other side of the lab, put on his white lab coat, and took down a stopper bottle labeled DMSO. To Branden he said, "You can't possibly know what you're doing, Mike."

"One doesn't swab out the spigot on a Barnsted water purifier, Dick. That was your mistake. It's hard enough to get pure water, without introducing unnecessary impurities. So, you had your poison on that Q-Tip. I figure you wanted that water sample to be doctored up just the right way, before you gave it to me."

Pomeroy said, "Didn't figure you'd notice, Mike." He took a small vial out of a drawer, put a drop of its contents into the bottle with DMSO, and mixed it in with a glass rod. The vial he put back in the drawer.

Branden nervously eyed the stopper bottle Pomeroy held, and said, "I've studied up on hydrolysis since we last talked."

"DMSO and water," Pomeroy said. "Must have been a lucky guess."

Branden shrugged, said, "Funny, too, that you would pay Sally Favor to isolate compounds that you never sent to a company for analysis. But, then, you always screen for toxicity with rats."

"You've been reading my lab books, Professor," Pomeroy said. "You'll no doubt have learned about this little gem," he said, tapping the bottle. "It's a synthetic derivative of a nasty little compound I found in Peru. I changed it a bit, so it's not quite so toxic as its parent compound, but now it does eventually hydrolyze, you see."

"Mixed with DMSO and water," Branden said, "there'd be nothing left to detect after, what, twelve hours?"

"Eight," Pomeroy said. "It was lethal for a good three hours, but became hydrolyzed after about eight hours. Depends on the concentration of water."

"Clever chemist," Branden said, and watched Pomeroy closely.

"There's no water diluting this sample, Mike," Pomeroy said, holding the bottle up to his eyes. "It's the perfect killing solution. Wouldn't take but a minute."

Branden backed up against the door, eyes fixed on the bottle in Pomeroy's hand. "Of course," Branden said, "I'll have to make a report of this to the sheriff."

"Of course," Pomeroy said. His eyes betrayed a certain embarrassment beneath his resolve. He sat down at his desk and twirled the bottle of poison solution in his fingers. "How many years have we taught together, Mike? Is it thirty years?"

"Something like that," Branden said, realizing what Pomeroy intended to do. He took a step forward.

Pomeroy held up his hand. "Don't Mike, it's over."

"We've been friends too long, Dick," Branden said.

"Right, we have. That's why you're not going to make me hurt you."

"Just give me that bottle," Branden said.

"Can't, Mike. What does it matter, anyway?"

"What about your work?" Branden asked, and moved closer.

"Mike, stop. I mean it. You can't take this bottle away from me without spilling some on you."

"Then set it down on the desk, Dick."

"You've got a future here, Mike. I don't. It's just that simple."

Quietly, Branden said, "You don't have to go out like this."

But Pomeroy wasn't listening. With a forlorn expression, he looked around his lab, and his gaze came to rest on the numerous lab books where he had recorded a lifetime of research. Then Pomeroy smiled, said, "See that some company gets my lab books and samples," and poured the DMSO solution into the palm of his left hand. As he rubbed his palms together, he slumped in his chair. He clutched his left arm to his chest, looked down at his hands, and laughed sardonically. The DMSO soaked into the skin. And Professor Dick Pomeroy dropped over dead on his desk.

45

Monday, November 4
10:15 A.M.

IN THE Chicago Renaissance Hotel, Bruce Robertson answered a knock at the door in his pajamas, and took a Fax delivery from the bellman. He sat in a chair in the corner of the room and switched on the light at a small table. Melissa Taggert stirred under the covers and asked, "What is it, Bruce?"

Robertson said, "Fax from Mike Branden," and started to read.

Said Missy, "Can you read it out loud?" and propped herself up on pillows.

Robertson scanned the page and said, "Sure."

Bruce,

I canceled my ten o'clock class, and to tell you the truth, I'm a bit stunned right now. But it's probably only 10:00 A.M. there, so I figure that gives me half a chance of catching you two love-birds still in bed.

Dick Pomeroy poisoned himself with the same mixture he used on Juliet Favor: DMSO plus a readily hydrolyzed plant extract that he discovered in Peru. He died in front of me, about two hours ago, from the same type of heart attack that killed Juliet Favor.

Sonny Favor has flown the coop. He took his jet back to New York yesterday, and isn't returning his calls. He told his sister that he smashed Favor's head in, after he found her sprawled on the end of her bed, very early Saturday morning. She had already died of a heart attack from Pomeroy's poison concoction.

Martha Lehman made some good progress with Evelyn Carson last night. As it turns out, she went back to the Favor mansion early Saturday morning, to confront Sonny about her pregnancy. (You'll recall that Daniel Bliss saw Sonny's Lexus out front, before dawn.) Martha says she saw Sonny carry the rugby trophy upstairs while she looked in a parlor window from the front porch. He didn't come back downstairs, so she went up, found Favor dead, and doesn't remember much after that, before Evelyn Carson found her Saturday morning, in the hall outside her office.

I got a pure water sample for Missy. My guess is that it won't show any of the small impurities that are present in either the DMSO mixture that Pomeroy prepared for Favor or the doctored water sample Pomeroy gave me yesterday. He had a perfect scheme to murder Juliet Favor, but I saw him swab out the spigot on his pure water source. That was his big mistake. He needed to introduce some of the poison to the water sample Missy would test, so that it would analyze the same as what she already had. He tried to make it look like he was just cleaning up a messy lab, and must have figured that I'd not take note of it. So, Missy, toxin analysis of Favor's blood wouldn't have shown anything, because the poison reacts with water eventually, to decompose. There also would not have been any poison left in the DMSO bottle by Saturday morning. If Sonny hadn't bashed her head in after the fact, no one would have suspected murder. Ironies abound.

Time to go. Arne Laughton has named me chairperson of a joint Faculty/Trustee committee to decide what to do with the money Juliet Favor left for the college in her will. I have many new friends waiting either in the hall or on the phone to talk to me about departmental budgets.

You kids be sure to have some fun.

Mike

Robertson folded the fax and laid it on the table. He came over to the bed, slipped in under the covers, and lay back with his hands behind his head. Missy snuggled up to the side of him, and draped her arm over his big chest. "I should have figured Dick Pomeroy would never have let his water purifier go down," she said. "Still, it was just traces in the water."

"What's that mean, hydrolyzed?" Bruce asked.

"It's any reaction with water. Usually it means something breaks down in water. Pomeroy mixed only about 7 or 8 percent water with Favor's DMSO, so that the poison would still be active when she likely would use it Friday night, but then it would have been hydrolyzed by Saturday morning, or at least by the time anyone got around to analyzing the DMSO. I thought I was seeing the kinds of small impurities you often find in untreated water. Instead, they were the hydrolysis products of Pomeroy's poison."

"You missed the poison?" Bruce teased.

"No. By the time I tested the mixture, the small amount of water had hydrolyzed the poison. Nothing was left but side products."

"You missed the poison!" Bruce said, and started tickling Melissa in the ribs.

AFTER lunch in bed, Bruce dressed in slacks and a sport coat, no tie.

Missy asked, "Time to dress, already?"

"I have plans for us, Missy. Several stops to make before dinner and the concert. Better suit up casual for now."

Missy dressed in a comfortable skirt and blouse outfit. Under the portico, Bruce asked for a certain doorman, tipped him twenty dollars, and winked. The doorman blew three short blasts on his whistle, and a black limousine pulled forward. Missy gawked at the long car, and said, "Bruce?"

Bruce held the rear door open, and motioned Missy in. As they drove off, he said to the driver, "You got the itinerary?"

"Yes, Mr. Robertson. It's all taken care of."

Missy looked wide-eyed at Bruce, and the sheriff smiled mischievously.

Missy said, "Does this have something to do with why you insisted we keep this date in the middle of a murder investigation?"

"That investigation wasn't going anywhere without Martha Lehman's statement. Since we'd be waiting for that for quite some time, I see no reason to have changed our plans."

"Oh is that right, Sheriff Robertson?"

"Yes it is, Coroner Taggert. Besides, I have plans for this day."

The first stop was the Sears Tower. On the observation deck, Bruce walked beside Missy as they slowly moved from one side to the next, gazing out over the vast city below. When they had circumnavigated the deck, Bruce produced a card with a single pink carnation on the cover. Inside, Missy read:

It seems like you can see the whole world up here, Missy. I'll never grow tired of it. This view is special for me because I first saw it with you. But, with all of the world laid out before me, I see nothing here that I don't see always in your eyes. There, I see all my dreams on the far horizons, the journey there certain in your eyes.

The next stop was Chicago's Shedd Aquarium. On the steps that face back toward the city, Bruce showed Missy the entire Chicago skyline. From the breast pocket of his long overcoat, he produced another card, the front a single red rose.

This is our skyline, Missy. It has been for me at least, since you first brought me here—on our first trip together after my burns had healed. You showed me this skyline at night, sparkling with a million city lights. You called those lights the promise that I could come through the burns. That I could come through the depression that has stalked me all my life. The promise that we could always love each other. It was that night that I started taking my medicine again. That night, that you showed me a life that could be whole and unblemished. A night of lights and stars. And promise. It was the night when I first knew that I loved you.

The last stop was the Art Institute of Chicago. They checked their coats after standing in a long line, and Bruce led Missy past dozens of masterpieces to a room where a bench sat in front of two giant canvases by Gerhard Richter. They sat on the bench for a long time, Bruce quiet, Missy wondering.

When Bruce did finally say something, he spoke haltingly at first. His voice cracked, and he had to clear his throat and start again.

"These are my favorite paintings, Missy, these Richters. Of all the ones we have seen together, these two speak to me the most. I love the way Richter has put a thousand magnificent hues on the canvas, as if the facets of countless perfect diamonds had cast their brilliance into the paint. That's you, Missy. All wonderful color, brightness, and life. Then that pale over-smearing of white is me. I thought, at first, that Richter was crazy. The overlay can't be meant for the colors underneath. The second obscures the first. Diminishes it, somehow. But, it's there, Missy, and it works. A masterpiece. Like you and me. You the thousand brilliant colors. Me the clumsy, gaudy smear. I figure these paintings give me hope for us. Hope that I can find a way to overlay my life with yours, without quenching your beauty. That, perhaps, you wouldn't find it too odious to blend your life with mine. That you'd consent to hold your beauty against my plain and simple canvas. That, perhaps, if art is ever glorious, and miracles still are possible, that you'd consent to be my wife."

46

Monday, November 4
7:30 P.M.

JUST three days after Juliet Favor's murder, Dr. Evelyn Carson sat at Mike and Caroline Branden's kitchen table with a mug of coffee. Caroline had chosen the mug for her, and said it was her favorite, a New England scene of a historic dockside town, with seagulls perched on harbor buoys.

"She's doing much better," Evelyn said. "Talking about Sonny Favor, today, was a good start. As I was leaving her room, John Schlabaugh came in, wearing a new suit and tie, flowers in hand. He had a short haircut and a fresh shave. Looked handsome."

"Was Martha happy to see him?" Caroline asked.

"Seemed to be," Evelyn said. "I only stayed a minute."

"It's funny," Caroline said. She halted, thought, shook her head. "Well, it's just kind of strange, that's all. To think John Schlabaugh could be this good for her, now."

Evelyn said, "She needs someone who understands her. Someone who won't be scared off by the hard times to come."

"Does Schlabaugh understand that?" Caroline asked.

"I think he does," Evelyn said, optimistically. "Now, tell me, Mike," she continued. "Where did Pomeroy make his mistake?"

"Oh, it was a lot of things," Branden said. Caroline nudged him in the ribs, and he said, "OK," with a groan.

"I guess the first thing was the spigot on the ultra-pure water system. Pomeroy swabbed that out with a Q-Tip. Problem was, he shouldn't have swabbed it with anything. I took a few chemistry classes in college, and as hard as it was, then, to get pure water, one never introduced a foreign object to a sample."

"You didn't suspect Pomeroy before that?" Evelyn asked.

"Well, actually, I did. When I was in Missy's lab, she had one bottle of DMSO up on her shelf. It came from Favor's place. I had to wonder. Why only one bottle? Daniel Bliss put me onto that one, Sunday night. He said Juliet Favor had two empty bottles Friday night, and Pomeroy was supposed to have brought her one more. Favor actually used the third bottle before dinner, so there couldn't have been any poison in that one. But that would have been three DMSO bottles, anyway.

"I figure Pomeroy went up the rear staircase before he left that night, and put a doctored bottle in Favor's medicine cabinet, or somewhere. Then, he had to take all the other bottles with him to make sure she would use the doctored one. He would have known, from past intimate experience, that she always went to the medicine cabinet to brush her hair at night, or at least that is what I infer from what Mr. Bliss said. But, Pomeroy could have gone up or down either the front or the rear staircase without drawing attention to himself. My guess is that Missy Taggert is going to say she found the fourth bottle in the bathroom. Favor dismissed her guests, went upstairs, brushed her hair, dabbed on the poison, put the bottle back in the cabinet, stumbled to the end of her bed, and died face down on the covers. That's how Sonny found her."

Caroline asked, "But what made you suspect poison in the first place? Especially if Missy couldn't detect any poison in the one bottle she had?"

"Juliet Favor was a workout nut. Even Bobby Newell, who has muscles 'out to here,' thought her routine was rigorous. She should never have had a simple heart attack."

"OK," Caroline said. "What made you think it was Pomeroy? It can't have been just the swabbing thing with the water spigot. After all, Missy couldn't detect poison in the DMSO."

"Pomeroy told me himself. At the faculty meeting. He made a big speech about the hydrolysis of pesticides, as a means of making them biodegradable. That's what I remembered when I finally figured out about the water. He put precisely enough water in with Favor's DMSO to hydrolyze the poison slowly, but not so much that the concoction would lose its potency too fast. Pomeroy could not resist making a speech about the one clue that, correctly understood, would prove him a murderer. And it proves my rule about faculty meetings."

Caroline and Evelyn waited.

Branden explained. "Faculty meetings last way too long, because professors love too much to hear themselves talk."

47

Thursday, November 7
7:30 P.M.

THREE days later, the Brandens rented the fellowship hall at Cal Troyer's church building and invited all of the officers and staff of the sheriff's office to a party for Ricky and Ellie Niell, and for Bruce Robertson and Melissa Taggert. The gathering served as an opportunity for a belated wedding shower for the Niells and an engagement party for the sheriff and the coroner. Simple refreshments of cake and punch were served, and the greatest attention was given to the gifts for Ricky and Ellie. Several toasts were made, congratulating either one or both of the couples. As the party moved along, Bruce Robertson found the professor at one of the back tables, and he took a seat there, next to his friend.

"You had it all wrapped up for us, Mike, by the time Missy and I got back from Chicago," Robertson said.

Branden sipped punch, nodded, and smiled.

Robertson said, "Now, how's 'bout filling me in on the motive."

"The motive was secondary," Branden said. "I figured out the 'how' first. Remember, we said early on that motive wouldn't solve this one."

"Right. Too many motives," Robertson said. "It could have been anyone, for nearly any reason."

"So, the motive was actually fairly obscure," Branden said. "Plain enough, once I had the facts, though."

"Enlighten me," Robertson said.

"First, Phillips Royce had Juliet Favor convinced that the sciences got too much money compared to the humanities. That's been his big kick for some time now. So, she was thinking about pulling out of grant support for science projects like Pomeroy's."

"I hope you're gonna tell me there was more to it than that."

"She was also going to sell him out on his industrial connections. Pomeroy had a sweet deal under the table with several firms, but the biggest was with her Yabusan Pharmaceuticals, in Tokyo. He was pulling down something like $70,000 per year by sending them processed natural products he found in Peru. He'd do all the key extractions in his lab in Peru—and that was paid for by Yabusan Pharmaceuticals, by the way—and ship the pasty extracts back here for analysis and workup."

"What can you do with something like that?" Robertson asked.

"It's a standard method, Bruce. How do you think they found Taxol, penicillin, all that stuff?"

"Seventy thousand a year for plant goo?"

"If you want to look at it that way, yes. He'd separate all the compounds and then screen each batch for undue toxicity. No point sending out toxins for drug testing. That he did with rats. Things that weren't toxic got sent to Tokyo for further analysis."

"Sounds like a tough way to do business."

"Like I say, it's a standard method. You know, the race to test the rainforest before it disappears. Anyway, Favor was considering two or three moves that would have put Pomeroy out of business. Mostly, she was going to shut down his lab in Peru. And she had started negotiations to sell Yabusan Pharmaceuticals, so Sonny Favor wouldn't have so much on his plate when he came into the family businesses."

"So, Pomeroy was takin' it on the chin," Robertson said. "How'd he know about it all?"

"He was on the board at Yabusan, but my guess is Favor told him outright. They used to be lovers, and she would have found some special satisfaction in watching him squirm. More, though, I think she really bought Phillips Royce's pitch for the humanities. She wanted to be chairperson of the board of trustees, but Arne Laughton had successfully blocked that appointment. So, instead, she saw a chance to change the nature of the institution another way. By changing her donations."

"Mike," Robertson teased. "I don't get the impression you liked her plan too much."

Branden shrugged. "People with a lot of money are accustomed to power and privilege."

"No doubt a reason," Robertson said, "why you and I are still making car payments each month."

"Don't get started on that one again, Bruce," Branden said, while trying to manage a frown.

Robertson laughed and held his hands up, surrendering. "Now, watch this," he said, and winked.

Getting up from the table, Robertson came forward to stand next to Missy. He clinked a fork against a glass to get everyone's attention. "Thank you all," he said, "for this party. It's real touching, and all, but Missy and I plan to get married in Las Vegas, so none of you can torment me at our wedding."

There were raucous protests and catcalls.

"You'll get over it," Robertson said.

Branden stood up in the back of the room and started clapping. Soon, everyone had joined him. Robertson, embarrassed, slipped his arm into Missy's and headed for the door.

As they were putting on their coats, three people eased into the room, unobserved by most, and stood along the wall. Cal Troyer saw them, and motioned to Branden. The professor caught Caroline's eye, and they met Cal with the three newcomers. The whole group of six ducked circumspectly through a door into the quiet sanctuary of the church.

Evelyn Carson took down the hood of her coat, and John Schlabaugh and Martha Lehman unzipped their coats and stood awkwardly, waiting for someone to talk.

223

Caroline took Martha's hands in hers gently and asked, "How are you, Martha?"

Martha checked Evelyn Carson's expression and said, "We're going to keep the baby."

John Schlabaugh nodded his agreement, and watched Caroline's eyes for a reaction.

Caroline looked first at her husband and then at Evelyn Carson. She studied the resolve in Schlabaugh's expression, smiled, and said, "Congratulations, then." She looked down to Martha's left hand, saw a diamond ring there, and added, "On both counts."

Branden saw relief in John Schlabaugh's eyes. To Martha, who was smiling, he said, "When you're ready to go back to school, your scholarship will still be there."

Evelyn said, "See, Martha, I told you so," and Martha teared up.

"I thought I had blown it, so bad," Martha said.

Caroline reached out for her, embraced her, and said, "You be happy, Martha Lehman. You just make sure you can be happy."

Back in the fellowship hall, Professor Branden made the announcement of the Lehman-Schlabaugh engagement, and many congratulations followed.

Martha took Caroline aside and spoke softly. "John is good for me," she said. "Don't worry. He's helping me remember."

Caroline started to speak, but Martha cut her off. "In all my dreams, nightmares really, there has been a man from whom I could not escape. I am a child, maybe five years old, and he is fast, strong, cruel, and dressed in blue and black. He is the blue shadow of my nightmares.

"Now, I understand that this man was real. I had forgotten about what he did to me when I was so young, because I was too young to face the truth. The nightmares are real, Caroline. They really happened. I know that, now. I can face them. Dr. Carson says I can.

"And that's what we're working on. John is there to hold me, when I wake up screaming in a child's voice. He is there, in sessions with Dr. Carson, to help me remember. Now, Dr. Carson says I have remembered only some of the times that man hurt me, but I have to be able to remember them all. It's going to take time. The last things I remember will be the worst. But, that's how I'll get better. By remembering, so that man can't hurt me anymore, in my mind. God has given me the meaning of the blue shadows now, so that I can be free of them for good."

Sometime later that evening, Martha found the professor, seated by himself at a back table. She sat next to him and asked, "What will become of Sonny Favor?"

Branden thought for a long time before answering. "He has been asked to withdraw from Millersburg College."

Martha seemed neither surprised nor sad. "What about all his money?"

"He has to stay in school to keep it."

"But, where?"

"Oh, there are plenty of schools where someone with his means would be welcomed."

"I feel sorry for him, Dr. Branden."

"I know," Branden said.

"John says he has a hole in his heart. Says it is money that put it there. Calls it a pierced heart."

Branden saw genuine sorrow in Martha's expression. "I think that's probably right, Martha," he said.